Dead Man Limping

AXEL HATCHETT MYSTERY VOL. 1

Steven LeRoy Nelson

BLOOD AND THUNDER PRESS

BLOOD AND THUNDER PRESS
3612 Sheffield Lane
Colorado Springs, CO 80907
www.bloodandthunderpress.com

ISBN: 1940469007
ISBN-13: 978-1940469003

To my wife, Georgeanne, with love.

1

The Ravencamp case had a stink about it from the very beginning, and it wasn't Rita Ravencamp's perfume.

She was all right, at least she looked it. Too tall maybe, and nervous and jittery. You could see it in her eyes, the way they darted around my shabby office as if tracking the flight of a frenetic fly. Which was certainly possible, but not likely. There was no buzzing And you could see her nervousness in her fingers, the way her pointy painted nails drummed against the sides of the pricey reptilian handbag she clutched in her lap.

I gave her a good looking-over, not too obviously, I hope, while she sat very upright in the uncomfortable client's chair across the desk from me. The waved red hair, multiple curves and sweetly undersized nose were okay. She took a cigarette from a slim gold case, and I suavely lit it with a wooden kitchen match, then watched her smoke it while she told me her improbable story. She had a silken voice, but with a rusty edge to it.

"Well, Mr. Hatchett, I guess I better tell you the whole tale, right?"

"My name's Axe, to you and my friends. Just tell me the parts you think I need to know. Time is money, Mrs. Ravencamp. Your money."

"Rita. Please. I was happily married until my husband disappeared. That was in '53, so...two years ago, a little over. Perhaps you read about it in the papers. He was driving to one of his week-end golf tournaments. Roscoe was an avid golfer.

"He was on the river road between here and Wavering Haze. It was raining that day. He swerved going around a curve, maybe to avoid hitting a deer or something crossing the road, and his car slid off the embankment and into the river.

"I know this because another motorist was be-hind Roscoe and saw the whole thing. He stopped and wanted to help, but what could he do? The river wasn't deep at that point, but it was running fast. Roscoe's Packard was up to its roof in water. It had landed on some submerged rocks."

"And there was no sign of your husband in the river, swimming or drowning or whatever?" I asked this just to get my oar in.

"No, nothing but water. The man who wit-nessed the accident walked up and down the riverbank, but he couldn't find any sign of Roscoe. He finally drove to the closest house, somebody's summer cabin, and used their phone to call the Quartz Quarry police. They took care of the rest.

"The witness, I think his name was Chad Lomax, drove back to the accident site. He waited until the rescuers arrived. A police cruiser, an ambulance, a fire truck and a tow truck. There was also somebody from the newspaper, the Gladiator. I'm surprised you didn't read about it."

"I wasn't here two years ago. Go on with your story."

"Some brave fireman tied a rope around his waist and swam out to the car. The driver's door window was rolled down, but there was nobody in the car. The keys were still in the ignition."

"I would think so. Was your husband a good swimmer? Or was he a sinker, like me?"

"Roscoe was a natural athlete, though he didn't care for most sports. His older brother, Alvin, who you'll hear about in a minute, doesn't believe that Roscoe would have drowned. Not unless he hit his head on a rock or something."

"But he never showed up, huh? They never found his waterlogged corpse? I mean, the unfortunate man's remains were never recovered?"

"No, never. He just disappeared."

She crossed her legs, uncrossed them, crossed them again. It was quite a show for a country boy like me. She fished out another cigarette and waited for me to light it.

"They searched for days," she continued, "checking the riverbank for miles. They even went out in a boat and looked for pockets or pools where his body might have ended up. No luck. By that time I was hysterical, and Alvin was drinking hard. That's what he does when he's upset. I believe it took two tow trucks to haul Roscoe's Packard to dry land. It was pretty well ruined.

"I thought I'd at least get a decent life insurance settlement. But...since they never found his body, they can't prove he's dead. The life insurance company hasn't given me a dime. But you know what? Alvin never gave up hope. That's just the kind of guy he is. He's still convinced that his brother will show up again. Somewhere, somehow."

I leaned back in my squeaky swivel chair, made a steeple of my hands, pursed my lips, and frowned at the ceiling. I do this sometimes when I don't know what else to do.

"Mrs. Ravencamp, Rita, I'm a bit confused. I've been hired for missing persons cases before, but nothing quite like this. Why would you wait two years to come to me, or any private investigator? I have to disagree with your brother-in-law. Roscoe Ravencamp isn't going to show up again, ever. They might find his bones someday. Listen. I'll look into the matter for you, but I think you're wasting your time and money."

She put a crafty smile on her face and twinkled her green eyes at me.

"That's what the police believe. Just what you said. But they're wrong and I want you to prove it."

She leaned forward in her chair and looked at

me, hard. Her smile got bigger, and she turned the volume up on all her attractions. I started to sweat. After all, I'm only flesh and blood. Okay, flesh and fat and blood. And quite a bit of gristle.

"Here, I'll show you." She dipped into her purse again and came up with a couple of photos. She pushed them across the desk at me, and I noticed she still wore her wedding ring. "These were taken a couple of years before Roscoe's disappearance."

I looked them over. Both pictures had been taken by some amateur with a box camera. They showed a guy around my age, thirty-five or so, and ugly as unrepented sin. A bulbous head. Tangled eyebrows guarding a pair of eyes as expressive as a pair of cocktail onions. The nose of a boxer. A very unsuccessful boxer. He wore thick horn-rimmed glasses, and a smile that would have looked right at home on a bulldog.

To complete his beauty he wore a chin about three feet long, with a cleft down its center that looked as long and deep as the bread slot on a toaster. The second picture showed the same mug, but in profile, with a big cigar clamped in its teeth.

"That's Roscoe," Rita explained unnecessarily. "I think you'll agree he has a distinctive face. You wouldn't easily confuse him with someone else."

"I'd have to agree with you on that. Does his brother Alvin look at all like him?"

"Not the tiniest bit. I grew up with them. And aside from their being about the same size and shape, there weren't many similarities. Roscoe looked like his mother, while Alvin favored his father. You wouldn't have guessed they were brothers, and only two years apart at that, even before Roscoe took up boxing while he was in the army. He had his nose broken five or six times. He wasn't a very good fighter, but I think he enjoyed it."

She dipped into her purse again and pushed another couple of photos across the desk, then smiled expectantly. They showed the same guy, but at a greater distance, and the light wasn't very good. One picture was even a little blurred. But it was the same ugly face all right. He looked paler, a little older. He had picked up two new scars. One on his massive forehead, and the other on his neck, a little below the jaw. He wore the same, or similar, horn-rimmed glasses

"Those pictures were taken last week," said Rita. "In town here. In fact, not many blocks from where we're sitting right now. Alvin took them. He's not much of a photographer, as you can see, and he was a bit nervous. Who wouldn't be, under the circumstances?"

"It doesn't make sense." I could hear the irritation in my voice. "Your husband drowns in a river, more than likely, over two years ago, and his remains are never recovered. Then he suddenly pops up again, alive, and he doesn't bother to contact his wife or brother. Why would he behave like that?"

"Alvin and I are wondering the same thing. There's that scar on his forehead that wasn't there before. We think maybe the head injury affected his mind, gave him amnesia or something."

"Possibly, though most cases of amnesia occur in movies, not real life. You said Alvin took both of these pictures in front of a building not far from here. Did he talk to his brother? I mean, why just take his picture?"

"Alvin tried to talk to Roscoe the first day he spotted him, but he ran away. Or, I should say, limped away. He appears to have hurt his leg as well as his head. I think — we think — Roscoe doesn't just have a regular case of amnesia, like in the movies, but something more complicated. It's like his memories are all scrambled. We think maybe he's confused and believes he's back in the war, behind enemy lines. He's hiding. He thinks we're the enemy. All of us.

"Of course we're only guessing. It'd take a real doctor to make a proper diagnosis. We need to find him before we can help him. That's why I came to you."

"I'm flattered," I said, offering a smile I hoped looked genuine. "Have you gone to the police with this story?"

"Yes, and they said they'd look into it. I don't think they really believed us. They listened to our story, looked at the pictures, asked questions. But I got the impression they thought we were out of our heads, or playing some sort of joke. We've called to talk to them since, and they never have any news. One officer even assured me that every one of us has a double somewhere. But what are the chances of Roscoe's double showing up right here in Quartz Quarry? The idea's absurd really. And another one — some desk jockey — asked if I realized it wasn't illegal for a man to just disappear. In other words, it's not police business. And to think our tax dollars are going to such a useless police force!"

"Sure. Makes me glad I never pay my taxes. Uh, that was a joke. So, if I'm understanding you correctly, you want to hire me to do what the cops won't or can't do. Nose around the neighborhood and see if I can track down and capture Roscoe Ravencamp. Right?"

Rita didn't like that. She gave me a look that should have shriveled me up like the Wicked Witch of the West. But I'm a tough guy, and her deadly stare only gave me a mild heart attack.

"You make him sound like some sort of wild animal. I hope you have more respect for the man I married than that. Still," she sighed a pleasant, breathy sound, "I suppose you have to look at him that way. I mean, if he's out of his head he could be dangerous. And it doesn't help that he has a gun."

That got my attention.

"A gun? How do you know he has a gun?"

"I'm only assuming, really. You see, Roscoe always kept a pistol, a forty-five from the war, in the glove compartment of his car. When his Packard was recovered from the river the gun was no longer there."

"Wait a minute. You think that while he was drowning your husband decided to take his automatic with him in case there was something in the great hereafter that needed shooting?"

"No, not like that. But Roscoe always had a lot of presence of mind. He may have taken the gun with the idea of signaling with it, or something. I only know that when the car was searched the gun was gone. And I doubt if a trout took it, Mr. Hatchett."

"Funnier things have happened. Tell me exactly what you want me to do, Mrs. Ravencamp."

"Oh, let's not both sulk. I'm sorry I was cross with you, but I counted on your being more open-minded than the police."

"I am. Trust me."

"Well, here's what Alvin and I want you to do. Actually, we've already done a lot of your leg work for you. We've asked around, and shown Roscoe's picture to people. Shop owners, waitresses, taxi drivers. No one's seen him. Oh, and that reminds me, I have further proof that Roscoe is alive and in town."

She made another trip to the reptile purse. This time she brought out a perfumed lace hanky, the sort of useless item ladies carry. I'm sure they'd never blow their noses in one. It was all wadded up, and when she unwrapped it, she revealed a big man's ring. Heavy gold, black onyx and diamonds. Tasteless but expensive. Rita handed it to me and I saw that the diamonds formed the initials RR.

"That's Roscoe's signet ring. He was wearing it when he disappeared. We found it in a pawn shop in town and redeemed it."

"What were you doing in a pawn shop? Are you telling me you and your brother-in-law went around to all the pawn shops in town looking for things Roscoe might have sold?"

"Yes. It was Alvin's idea, and a good one as it turns out. Alvin figured Roscoe might have to raise some money somehow. Doesn't this ring practically prove that my husband is alive and living here?"

"No, not really. Somebody might have come across it wherever your husband's unrecognizable corpse washed up. As far as it's being two years later, that ring may have passed through a number of hands and many pawnshops since it was found."

She had a look of mild, poisonous, irritation in her eyes.

"You're a hard man to please."

"That's to your advantage," I said. "You don't want to hire some chump who swallows every story whole, do you?"

"Of course not. But you'll have to believe in Roscoe's return to the living if you're to give this matter the attention it deserves. Can you promise you'll do that?"

I squirmed a little in my swivel chair, causing it to emit a series of squeaking sounds that would have done any rat proud. I couldn't honestly tell this redhead with money that I believed her story. She might as well have hired me to track down the Easter Bunny and bring back its eggs.

But at that very moment, my two worst guardian angels, poverty and curiosity, whispered in my ear that I was broke and that this case of the limping dead man was actually kind of interesting. I opened my mouth to tell Rita that I'd take the case.

I wasn't fast enough. My third guardian angel, my best, a sniveling toddler, warned me that pursuing a missing man who had a head injury and a gun might not be healthy.

"Can I have a couple of days to think about it?" I asked.

She shook her head. "I don't see what there is to think about. Either you can do the job or you can't. You were recommended to me by someone who obviously has poor judgment. There are other private investigators in town."

"Yeah. I know them. They're bums. They charge too much, they pad their expenses, and really, they don't have a whole lot of brains. I wouldn't hire one of them to find my hat if it was on my head."

"Are you telling me, in your own odd way, that you'll take the job?"

I took a moment to contemplate the difference between starving and being shot. It appeared to be a toss-up.

"Okay, I'll do it. It will take me a few minutes to type up a contract. Then we'll have to haggle over the fee. In the meantime, can I offer you something to drink? I've got some coffee on the hot plate, but it's a little past its prime. How about some water? I know where there's a water cooler in an office down the hall. Would you like some water?"

I fed paper and carbon into my vintage Remington and, using both my index fingers, typed up my simple standard contract.

"No water?"

"I'm fine, thank you. But before I sign that contract, I want to make certain that you know exactly what we want you to do. You talked about 'capturing' my husband. I don't think that's a good idea. I don't want anybody to get hurt. I don't want your blood on my hands, quite frankly. And I don't want Roscoe injured.

"Here's what I want. Collect enough evidence of my husband's continued existence to convince the police to take the matter seriously and to act accordingly. That's basically it. I'll have Alvin show you the old apartment building where we think Roscoe's been hiding out. Maybe you can go on stakeout there. Isn't that what you call it, a stakeout?"

"Sure. I like stakeouts. They're fun. Like camping, but without the hotdogs and the bears. Let me ask you, do you think your husband's nocturnal? Or does he still come out in the daytime?"

"I'm not sure. The three times Alvin's seen him it was in the early evening. But that really doesn't tell us anything, does it?"

"That's okay. It's just that if I'm going to rifle through his digs I don't want to be there when he walks in and says, 'Hi, honey, I'm home.' That could be awkward. Besides, I don't want to spook him into moving someplace else."

"You and Alvin can check out the place together. Safety in numbers and all that. But do be careful. I don't want you getting any closer to Roscoe than you have to in order to get a few good pictures. As for Roscoe getting 'spooked' into finding a new place to hide, that's all right. I've already explained — and I'm telling you one last time — your job is not to catch and detain my husband. That will be a job for the police.

"You are being hired to collect evidence, as much as possible, that my husband is alive and living in Quartz Quarry. This is all you are to do." She gave me a smile more full of teeth than warmth. "When can you start? Today?"

"Absolutely."

She signed the contract, then wrote down some phone numbers for me. Hers and Alvin's. Both their home phones and their work phones. Rita ran a little art shop. Alvin was a locksmith.

"I'll have Alvin call you today or drop by your

office, if that's all right. If you don't hear from him, give him a call yourself."

She bid me a fond farewell, and the smile she gave me was much nicer than the earlier one. Her perfume lingered for a little while, but it didn't stand a chance in my odoriferous office.

Left to myself, I lit up a cigar about as tasty as a damp railroad flare. I sat at my desk and smoked and thought until I couldn't stand it anymore. I've had clients lie to me before. It's one of the things you have to watch out for in my line of work. I didn't know what was going on with Rita and her ghost of a husband, but it sure as hell wasn't your average missing person's case. I needed to find out a couple of things before I got in any deeper.

For starters, I wanted to find out if there was any chance that Roscoe Ravencamp faked his own death. People have done that before, but they don't usually come back to the place they disappeared from. And I wasn't buying any of that "Where am I? Who am I?" amnesia crap.

I decided I needed to make a visit to the offices of our noble newspaper, the Gladiator. I could spend a little time in their morgue, and maybe talk to a reporter friend of mine, if he was available.

I grabbed my hat, locked up my home-away-from-home, and headed around to the back of the building where I park my noble steed, my Hudson Hornet. This car was the only thing of value that I had left from what I thought of as the old, prosperous times.

2

The building that housed the Gladiator was a big pile of concrete with a vaguely Roman appearance. At least it looked old enough to be Roman. Once inside I was greeted by a sour receptionist who grudgingly allowed me to peruse the morgue. It was in the basement.

I found what I was looking for in pretty short order. I counted back two and a half years and hauled about a year's worth of news over to a scarred wooden table. I didn't have to look long before I came across the first reference to Roscoe's unfortunate accident, under the irreverent headline, 'Local Motorist Makes Waves.' There were more articles, spread out over a period of a couple of weeks, and then the incident had become old news.

What Rita had given me was pretty much the straight dope. I didn't learn anything new except for a little history regarding Roscoe's meteoric rise from construction crew flunky — right after the war — to successful partner in a lucrative local real estate firm.

I jotted down the partner's name. I also wrote down the name of the guy who had been driving behind Roscoe on that fateful day two years ago. Rita had remembered right, the guy's name was Chad Lomax. Further, I got the name of the tow truck driver who showed up on the first day, and the company he worked for.

Having found everything I could in the morgue, I climbed the stairs all the way to the second floor where they kept the newsroom. I waded through the cranky chaos until I found the desk of Barney Lever, my reporter friend, who had also penned the original "Local Motorist Makes Waves" article.

Barney was a short guy in his early forties, with a fringe of curly ginger hair on an otherwise bald head. When he saw me he stood up and offered me a clammy hand to shake.

"What kind of trouble you in now, Axe?"

"No trouble. I'm just trying to do my job. And you? Still prosperous as ever?"

"Sure. Everything's the hunkiest of doriest, as they say. Can I do something for you, or did you just drop by to remind me that your birthday's coming up?"

"I want to ask you about a car accident."

"One that's already happened?"

"Yeah. Couple of years ago. Guy named Roscoe Ravencamp drove off the road into the river."

"Sure, I remember. Guy thought he was driving a submarine. The kind of mistake anybody could make."

"Do you remember it or not?"

"I remember. Crystal clear. What a shame — what a crying shame. That Packard he baptized was one sweet ride. Some folks don't appreciate what they've got."

"Would you like me to give you a minute to yourself so you can shed a bitter tear?"

"No, I got ahold of myself now. What do you want to know? That accident was a couple of years ago, you realize."

"Could it have been faked? I mean, could Ravencamp have set it up to look like his final exit, then snuck off to Coney Island or some other tropical paradise?"

Barney motioned for me to sit in the wobbly wooden chair next to his desk. He offered me a stale jelly doughnut, but I don't care much for artifacts.

"Maybe." Barney shrugged. "I mean, they never found the body, and that's enough to make a guy like me suspicious. But I could never dig up anything on that angle. For starters, there was that witness."

"Could have been bribed."

"Sure, but who would trust anybody that much? Besides, what's in it for Ravencamp that would make him want to disappear? I could never figure out a reason. Happily married to a beautiful wife. Partner in a business making boxcar-loads of money. Healthy as a turkey the day before Thanksgiving. Why would he give that up to disappear somewhere? He didn't owe back taxes or have any gambling debts that I could ever uncover. An affair? I figure he might have played around a little. But he didn't have to leave town for that. Maybe he knocked-up his secretary or something. But money usually takes care of things like that.

"I admit Ravencamp was kind of a hobby for me for a while. But the cops said nothing looked suspicious, and the witness got up on his hind legs when I questioned him, so I really don't think he was part of some scheme."

"Could someone have murdered Ravencamp, buried him in the trees somewhere, then driven his car into the river and maybe swam to shore?"

Barney gave me a look of the purest pity.

"These are people we're talking about, Hatchett. People are dumb, they screw up, they get caught because they aren't good enough to get away with even simple crimes. Tarzan couldn't do what you just described. Either it was a real accident, and the body got sucked into an underwater cave, or he decided to make it look like that, in which case he pushed the car off the embankment and into the river.

"Now why don't you leave me alone and go hunt up that witness? He still lives here. He's the principal at Quartz Quarry Elementary. If you can prove he's a crook, the kids will be really happy. His name is — "

"I know his name. You don't have to tell me everything. Thanks for the information. I'll see you around."

"Good luck, Scoop. You sure you don't want this doughnut?"

I told my friend goodbye and headed for my Hudson.

It was late August. School wouldn't be starting for another week or so, but I was hoping a big shot like the principal would already be ensconced at the school, figuring out new ways to torment his hapless captives. I was in luck. Lomax and his secretary were in residence.

Principal Lomax was a pompous s.o.b. I found him in his office where he was very importantly doing nothing at all. The "In" box on his desk was empty. So was the "Out" box. He sat in a high-backed oak swivel chair, and rested his fat folded hands on the leather blotter of his big oak desk. He eyed me the way a spinster librarian would eye someone she caught using a lovely leather-bound book for a drink coaster.

"State your business, Mr.?"

"Hatchett."

"Really? I haven't any time. Really, I don't know why Miss LeMink allowed you to get past her desk."

"I used the old boot-in-the-face trick. She wasn't expecting it."

"Really? Come on, why are you here?"

"I'm an investigator. I'd like to ask you a few questions about a car accident you witnessed a couple of years ago."

He suddenly waved his arms around like he was clearing a path through a flock of birds. "Not again," he shouted. "This is a dead subject for me. Get out of my office. And on your way out, send Miss LeMink to me. What an outrage. Why can't you just give the poor woman her money?"

"Miss LeMink?"

"Of course not! The widow. Mrs. Ravencamp. I cannot believe the greed of insurance companies. I will not be questioned on this matter again. This must be the hundredth time!" He pointed at a big wooden spanking paddle hanging on the wall. "Do you see that? Do you see those holes drilled through it? When someone is paddled, those holes cause blisters to form. You go back to your boss, whoever he is, and tell him about that paddle."

I thought about sticking to my guns and bullying this idiot into giving me some answers, but I doubted he actually had anything to tell me. I had to agree with Barney Lever: if this arrogant jerk had been any part of a scheme for disappearing Roscoe Ravencamp, he'd been duped into the role of witness. So all I said to Lomax was, "Thank you for your time. I'll send Miss LeMink in to you to wipe the sweat from your care-worn brow."

I got up and left. As I passed through the outer office I gave Miss LeMink what I hoped was a look of heart-felt sympathy, but she didn't see it. She was busy typing.

The sun was shining pretty hard by the time I got back to my car. It was close to noon, and my stomach was telling me that it was time to refill the tank. Since I wanted to get the taste of Lomax out of my mouth first, I decided to drive to the towing company, Herb's Hook Shop. It was on the edge of town. I'd seen it before, so I pointed the Hornet in its direction and hit the gas pedal.

Herb had picked a nice spot for his garage. It was right on the highway with plenty of open land around it to furnish parking space for a variety of seriously-wrecked vehicles in various stages of rust and corrosion. The garage itself was a square building made of concrete blocks, painted white, with a couple of jaunty horizontal red stripes up near the roofline.

I parked the car and walked over to the service bay area. A couple of white-and-red tow trucks sat idly to one side of the building. The big service bay doors were open. Inside was the smell of grease, cleaning solvent, and new rubber. Along one wall were stacks of tires, some wrapped up in brown paper tape.

There were two lifts, one empty, the other holding up a big maroon Buick. A guy in white coveralls was standing under the Buick, torturing it with a noisy impact wrench, and cursing loudly enough for me to hear over the racket. I waited for him to let up a moment, then stepped forward and introduced myself. He had thick hairy arms with some blue tattoos of a nautical nature showing through the fur. There was a streak of shiny grease in his blond crew-cut. A patch on his left breast pocket said 'Herb' in embroidered letters. The man himself.

"What can I do for you, Mr. Hacksaw?"

"Hatchett. Call me Axe. I'll be needing some new rubber on the Hudson out there pretty soon, but right now I just want a little information. Can you spare a moment?"

"Sure. I don't mind taking a break from this rust bucket. I'm getting some coffee, you want some?"

He led me into an office with filing cabinets and a desk, behind which sat a fuzzy-haired damsel who might have been Mrs. Herb. She was frowning and punching numbers into an adding machine.

"Lura here cooks the books for us," Herb said, grinning at the girl.

"Fat lot of good that'd do you," said Lura, not even looking up.

Herb took two coffee mugs, one gold, one green, from a shelf above a gleaming electric percolator. He filled both mugs and handed me the green one.

"Sugar? I can't offer you milk because there's no icebox."

"I take it black, thanks."

I watched Herb pour about half a sack of sugar

into his coffee while I tasted mine. It was black all right. And thick. And oily. I've had worse. I've made worse. We drank our coffee standing up while I told Herb what I wanted to know.

"Sure, I remember. That Ravencamp guy drove right into the river. His tires were probably getting bald, or he needed new brake shoes. Say, that was a good two years ago. I don't remember a whole lot about it. Why're you asking?"

"Insurance," I said, and instantly regretted it. I watched as the blood darkened Herb's poorly shaven face. A scar near his eye I hadn't noticed before showed stark white against his flushed skin.

"You one of those insurance creeps?" He practically spat the words at me.

"Just the opposite," I hurried to assure him. "I represent the widow. She still hasn't been paid her husband's life insurance because the body never showed up."

"The guy went into the river! What's he been doing, holding his breath for two years?"

"I'm with you, pal. But you know how these insurance companies are. I'll tell you what happened. A few weeks ago they found some old bones near Echo River, only a mile or so from where Ravencamp's car did a belly flop. They turned out to be the bones of a big raccoon, but it got these insurance guys scared. Now they're trying to prove that the accident was faked so that Ravencamp could slip away to the high lonesome and start a new life. Can you believe these guys? The widow's pretty ticked off. She's hired me to check things out, and show that the accident was just that: an accident. After all this time I'm not sure what I can find out. I'm clutching at straws."

I was making up things as I went along. I really should practice my lies in advance. But Herb didn't question my silly story. He was too intent on helping out the poor widow. I could tell.

"You mean you think there might have been something about the car that could help you prove the accident was legit? I don't know, I'm not the guy to talk to. Back then I was the only real mechanic here. I let my other guys handle the towing, so I never even saw the car. Benji towed it some place. Some lot the police department keeps, I think. You could ask him. Benji still works here, but I sent him to lunch about the time you got here. You could wait, but he takes long lunches."

"Could you tell me where he might have gone to lunch? I could use a bite myself. Would he mind talking to me?"

"No. Benji likes to talk."

Lura snorted, and for the first time looked up from her adding machine. I noticed she was cross-eyed. "I'll say Benji likes to talk," she said, somewhat nasally. "I just wish he liked to work." She went back to her adding machine. Herb looked at me and shrugged.

"Benji likes Thelma's Chicken Coop," he said. "I don't know if it's the food so much as the waitresses, but the food's not bad."

"I know the place. It's right down the road. Thanks for your help."

"Sure. Good luck. Come back when you need those new tires."

3

A few minutes later I pulled into the gravel drive belonging to Thelma's Chicken Coop and parked in back where there was an honest-to-god chicken coop full of laying hens and a few doomed fryers.

The restaurant itself was a rambling shed-like structure with lots of short windows and some cheery flower boxes devoid of flowers. Inside was a long lunch counter and a bunch of small tables. The menu, surprisingly, featured a lot of egg dishes.

I looked down the row of lunch counter stools and spotted a guy wearing white coveralls like Herb's. There was a half-eaten slice of lemon pie in front of him, so I figured he'd reached the dessert phase of his meal. There was an empty stool next to him, so I hurried over and sat on it, placing my hat on the counter next to me.

A freckled waitress with nicely undulating hips came over and asked me what I'd have. I ordered two egg sandwiches with cheese and ham, and a cup of coffee. I turned to Benji, a small man with the face of a good-natured barn rat. He was paying less attention to his pie than to the retreating backside of our waitress.

"Why don't you go ahead and ask her out?" I said by way of introduction.

He turned to me with a startled look on his rodent muzzle. "I could never do that," he whispered, intensely. "A swell dame like her? She'd laugh me through the floorboards."

I shrugged. "Suit yourself. My name's Hatchett. I'm an investigator. Your boss told me I'd probably find you here. I've got a couple of questions for you, if you don't mind."

The startled look came back to his face. "Herb sent you to me? What'd I do?"

"Nothing. Relax."

The waitress brought me my food, and I wolfed down half a sandwich before I returned my attention to Benji, grease dripping from my chin. He remembered the Ravencamp accident.

"I wasn't driving the tow truck that day. I was riding shotgun with Sonny Draper. Sonny ain't with us no more."

"Dead?"

"No, he just ain't with us. He packed up and moved to Oregon, or some damn place. Just as well, because Sonny liked to keep a pint of hooch in the glove compartment of the wrecker he drove. In the morning that bottle would be full, but by quitting time it'd be a dead soldier. Herb knew about it and was getting ready to can Sonny, but then Sonny up and quit."

I bit into my second sandwich and some egg yolk squirted out and went into my coffee, which reminded me to drink it before it got cold.

"Was Sonny boozing the day you went to pull Ravencamp's car out of the drink?"

"No, that was before. Before Sonny's wife ran off with that water softener salesman. He was sober that day, but what could we do? We had a tow truck, not a damn tug boat. We went out with two trucks later in the week and managed to drag that Packard up on dry land. We had to beat it up some to do it. And somebody could have drowned. Think of that, a tow truck driver drowning on the job! Sounds like something for a newsreel."

"That first day you went out, was the guy who witnessed the accident still there?"

"Yeah, he was there. Principal Pop-Goes-the-Weasel, or whatever his name is."

"Lomax. Did you talk to him?"

"No, I don't talk to that guy. My nephew goes to that school. When he accidentally tossed a brick through the window of the music room, old Lomax called the kid to his office and spanked him with a paddle the size of a lifeboat oar. There were holes drilled in it for making blisters. Can you believe it?"

I realized at this point that if I was to get any

useful information out of Benji it would take the better part of a month. I finished my lunch and made a hasty retreat.

I sat in my car in the parking lot trying to decide where I should go next. Of course, I could have saved time by just talking to people on the phone, but I don't care for that. I like to watch people when I talk to them. And I like to confront them in their own natural habitat. I learn a lot more that way than if I just squawk to somebody on the telephone. Besides, I'm no good at sitting at a desk all the time. And I like driving the Hornet.

After contemplating my heartburn for a few minutes, I went back inside Thelma's and borrowed a phone book. I looked up Roman and Ravencamp, the real estate firm. I decided it might be a good idea to talk to Roscoe's old partner, feel him out about the missing man's mental state right before he disappeared. I didn't expect Randell Roman to be all that talkative about his late friend, but you never know, and it was worth a try. I didn't call before I went over there, because I didn't want to be expected. I just jotted down the address and drove over there.

The offices of Roman and Ravencamp Real Estate were housed in an ugly, squat, cement-and-glass structure. It was out in the country, in the middle of a new housing project named Hazy Horizons, which was filling up with a rash of poorly-made one story homes of blond brick with brown roofs. Very festive. You could tell them apart by looking at the house numbers. I parked near one corner of the building, next to a dusty old Ford woody. There were only two other cars in the parking lot, one on each side of the wide glass entrance. One was a swell red Chrysler rag top. The other was a spanking new sapphire-blue Lincoln.

As I got closer to the front door, I saw the two signs on the wall in front of the cars. One said "Mr. Roman." The other said "Mrs. Roman." A charming touch that came within twenty degrees or so of warming my heart. I doubted if the Romans worked together. Husband and wife usually see enough of each other at home and don't want to mix business with pleasure. Perhaps, I thought, Mrs. Roman had brought money to the marriage and felt proprietary towards the business she'd helped her better half to purchase. But that wasn't at all the case, as I soon found out.

It was cool inside the office. Too cool. But air conditioning is the sort of thing businesses like to show off. It makes them look prosperous if they can keep the temperature in the sub-arctic range in the summer. The receptionist sat behind a desk no bigger than a sewing machine cabinet.

She was young and recently permed. She didn't have enough chin, but had other attributes to make up for it. She wore a sweater, but not just because she was a sweater girl. Her nose was as blue as an orphan's on Christmas. I introduced myself, but she wasn't impressed. I get that a lot. She informed me that Mr. Roman was busy in a meeting, and that I should make an appointment the next time instead of counting on luck.

"What about Mrs. Roman?" I asked, just to see what would happen. "Might she be available?"

Blue-nose muttered something under her breath. I thought it sounded like, "She sure used to be available," but I couldn't be sure.

"You'll have to speak up," I told her "My ears are only big on the outside. Did you say your lady boss was available, or not?"

That got a reaction, sort of a silent explosion.

"She's not my boss," she hissed at me "I went to high school with her."

"You and Mrs. Roman? Mr. Roman must have been quite a prodigy to have put together this business at such a young age."

"Mr. Roman," she said, still whispering fiercely, "is old enough to be his wife's father. Maybe even her grandfather. And the way he dotes on Charly is disgusting."

"Charly?"

"Charlene. Take right now, for instance. He has plenty of work to do, but when she showed up he dropped everything. They've been in there chatting and laughing, and who knows what all, for over an hour. He's got a bottle in his desk drawer and I'll bet they're having drinks right now. And snooty Charly acts like she doesn't even remember who I am, like we didn't go to school together for years. I'd quit this job if I could find another."

"Listen, I might be able to help you with that. I

know a lot of people. But why didn't you tell me what kind of a meeting was going on when I first came in?"

"Mister, I don't know you from Adam."

"It's easy enough to tell us apart. Adam's older than me, and his mustache is trimmed up better. I think he's got a better barber." I leaned over the desk a little. "Listen, sister, I'm just here to help out a poor widow, I swear. So couldn't you fix it so I can talk to Roman in private a few minutes?"

"Well, you'll have to wait until the princess leaves. I'll see what I can do. But don't tell me any more stories about starving widows."

"I didn't say she was starving. Gee, I hope she isn't."

"Take a seat, it might be a while. What was your name again?"

"Hatchett. You know, like the boy scouts carry. First name Axel. Like the part of the car they fasten the chain to when they pull you out of the mud."

"It's a silly name. I bet you made it up."

"No, my parents did. I don't know what they were thinking."

I sat down and leafed through a fishing magazine. I was deeply absorbed in an article on how to fool the wily brook trout when Roman's office door swung open. At first I only had eyes for his young wife. Anybody would have looked good in that expensive dress, but she wasn't just anybody. She was short and small boned, but she had a kind of a regal air about her. I bet Napoleon would have looked the same, if he'd been a girl and a real looker, but we'll never know.

"I'll see you to your car," said the big guy who held her by the arm. He was tanned and graying, though not as old by a long shot as the receptionist had indicated. He wore a well-cut blue suit that went well with his hair and his shiny black shoes. His necktie was another matter entirely, like something you'd win at a carnival by shooting a BB gun at a tin rabbit. Maybe the missus had given it to him.

He gave me an appraising politician's stare then looked quickly at his receptionist while she busied herself with paperwork. Roman finished the job of escorting his fair bride out the door and to her car, a walk of forty feet, total. I heard the purr of the sapphire Lincoln and then Roman reappeared, dabbing a bit of ruby lipstick from his mouth with a light blue handkerchief I'll bet was monogrammed.

Before he could say anything to her, the receptionist, whose name I intended to learn, looked up and said quite casually, "Mr. Roman, this is the Mr. Hatchett I told you about. He wasn't able to make an appointment, so he stopped by on the off chance you might have had a cancelation."

I liked this girl. She was twisting her boss around her teensy little pinky. For his part, he looked genuinely perplexed at this point. Before he could regain his bearings I stood up and offered my hand.

"I won't take up much of your time, I promise. I'm a private investigator. I've been hired by your late partner's widow, Mrs. Ravencamp, to aid her in recovering the money owed her by Mr. Ravencamp's life insurance representative."

Roman made an exasperated noise and I thought I was going to be thrown out on my ear. But it turned out his exasperation wasn't aimed at me.

"That damned insurance company," he raged. "You mean to tell me Rita still hasn't recovered her money from those bloodsuckers? Roscoe's been dead more than two years. I don't know how that insurance company can keep holding out."

"Actually, they've got a new angle that I'd like to discuss with you. In private, if that's possible."

I glanced meaningfully at the receptionist, who pretended to be paying no attention to us. Roman also looked at the girl, then motioned me into his office and closed the door behind us. The office was swell, almost as big as the reception area, with two large windows looking out on nothing in particular.

The plush carpet looked too expensive to walk on. There were some showy pictures on the wall that might have cost something. The furniture, and there was quite a bit of it, was all made of highly polished teak wood. Roman motioned me to a tall, comfy leather chair while he moved to his chair behind a desk that was only a little smaller than a milk truck. He clearly knew the value of appearances.

"Can I offer you a drink? I've got some pretty good scotch." He reached over and pulled out a desk drawer. "Or is it too early for you?"

"Actually, I'm thinking of going out for a nice steak dinner tonight, with maybe a couple of highballs to help it go down. So, no thanks. But by all means pour yourself one. I don't mind."

"Later," he said, closing the drawer. "Now tell me, what is Rita's insurance company up to now?"

"Well, they're wanting to prove it was suicide, that way they'll never have to cough up the dough."

"Suicide? I don't suppose you knew Roscoe?"

"No, sir, I'm relatively new in town. I never had the pleasure."

"Pleasure may not be the right word. Roscoe could be difficult, and he was quite a character. He was certainly one of the ugliest men I've ever known. Have you seen his picture?"

"Yes. I guess he had the kind of features you'd call rugged."

"Rugged? Wrecked would be more like it. A great advertisement for staying away from the sport of boxing. At least as a participant. How such a Halloween ghoul could attract a dream like Rita I'll never know. I don't know what he had. Drive? Pep? Something."

"You've done pretty well in that department yourself, I'd say. Not that I'm comparing your mug to Roscoe's, but that's quite an eyeful of a missus you've got, if you don't mind my saying so."

"Oh, yes. Charly's made me a very happy man. Expensive tastes, and a bit of a temper, but everything has its price as they say. But let's get back to this notion of Roscoe's committing suicide. Nothing could be less likely. I knew the s.o.b. pretty well. Believe me, he'd never have pulled down the curtain on his own show. He didn't climb his way to the top just so he could jump off."

"I believe you, of course, and Mrs. Ravencamp said very much the same thing to me. But how can we prove it wasn't suicide? Now that the insurance company appears to have decided that Ravencamp really and truly is dead, how do we kill this notion that his death was self-inflicted?"

Roman thought about it. While he was thinking, he lit up a cigar and offered me one. I was happy to accept. His cigars were much better than the kind I can afford. For one thing, they were actually made out of tobacco instead of ground-up crabgrass. We both sat and puffed for a while. I noticed two spots of color high on Roman's cheeks, and his eyes were close to glassy. I wondered how many nips of scotch he and the divine Charly might have shared. I was the one to break the silence.

"It'd be perfect if we could prove the car malfunctioned, but I guess it's way too late for that."

"I'll say. I don't even know where that Packard

36

ended up. I believe Rita sold it for a song to some guy who hoped to dry it out and get it running again. There's no telling where the car is now. Besides, Rita had that car all checked out. As far as the mechanic could tell there was nothing wrong with the tires, or the brakes, or anything."

"Why'd she want to find out? Just curious?"

He shrugged. "I've never thought about it. Perhaps she also thought it might be suicide."

"Or murder?"

"Murder?" Roman puffed so energetically on his cigar that a long finger of ash grew on it before he could tap it off in the ashtray. Part of the ash landed on his swell desk blotter, and he frowned at it while he told me just what he thought of the idea of his partner's having been knocked off. "Why would you come up with a cockeyed notion like that? Roscoe had some rough edges, and he no doubt made some enemies along the way, but murder?"

"Just an idea. If it was murder and we could prove it, that'd knock the whole suicide notion on its ear. Of course, it's always possible that the insurance company was right all along. Roscoe might not be dead. He might have planned the whole thing so he could disappear, for whatever reason."

"That's as crazy as the idea of his killing himself. Who'd want to disappear with Rita around? And, hell, the guy was successful. I ought to know."

He thought some more, and the rest of his cigar went the way of the city of Pompeii. "Disappeared, huh?" he finally said. "He was an odd duck, that's for sure. You could hardly get the guy to take a vacation. But, you know what? When he did take a couple of weeks off it'd be during hunting season. He'd go off in the woods all by himself, just him and his rifle, and he'd come back with nothing. No deer, no elk, no nothing.

"Roscoe was an Eagle Scout when he was a boy. One of the meanest ones that ever lived, I'm sure. But he learned how to track. And he was a sniper in the war. He knew how to shoot. But all he ever came back with from his hunting trips was a half empty box of cartridges."

The fancy teakwood intercom on his desk buzzed.

"Yes, Miss Fitzue?"

"Mr. Anderslaver is here for his two o'clock appointment."

"Wonderful. I'll be ready for him in a moment."

He stood up, so I stood up too. He extended his right hand, so I shook it.

"I don't feel I've helped you much, Mr.? Handaxe?"

"Close enough. You've helped me plenty. I just hope everything will work out for Mrs. Ravencamp."

"Me too. When you see her again, tell her I said hello."

He put a firm hand against my back and gently

propelled me through the office door he'd just opened. He exchanged me for Mr. Anderslaver, a tall, large-hipped man with a crew-cut and somebody else's suit.

I now had Miss Fitzue all to myself.

4

As soon as Roman's office door was closed once more, I made my move on the blue-nosed secretary. She appeared fairly disenchanted with her position, and I thought I might get her to spew some poison about her late employer, Roscoe Ravencamp. Of course, this was assuming she'd been working at the same job two years earlier.

I approached her tiny desk and stood waiting while she finished talking on the phone with someone. I really wasn't trying to eavesdrop, but I heard her mention a Sunset Hollow, which I figured must be a new housing development with all the amenities, or a new cemetery with all the amenities.

She finally hung up and gave me a darkly appraising look that very clearly told me that she didn't believe I'd fetch much at a flea market.

"I wasn't trying to horn in on your conversation," I explained. "I just wanted to have a few words with you before I go, if you don't mind."

"You're trouble, aren't you? What kind of snake oil were you selling to Mr. Roman?"

"I wasn't selling anything, really. I was only asking a few questions on behalf of my client, Mrs. Ravencamp. Were you working here when Mr. Ravencamp had his accident?"

"Sure. It was a real shock. But I'm kind of busy right now, you know? I really don't have time to answer your questions, whatever they are."

I sidled a little closer to her desk, and put on my best smile of gratitude, which, admittedly, isn't all that convincing. "I appreciate your getting me in to see your Mr. Roman the way you did," I said. "I'd like to return the favor. Say, do you like steak?"

"What? Steak? Listen, I need to get back to work."

"Sure, I understand. You're a busy girl. That's why I'm suggesting we talk later, maybe over dinner. But don't mistake my meaning. I'm not asking for a date. You think a guy with a mug like mine would ask out a swell girl like you?"

"Sure. The world's full of creeps. "

"Come on. Stop massaging that typewriter long enough to listen to me a second. All right?"

"No. We aren't eating steak together. I'm a busy gal and I got a boyfriend, though God knows he can't spring for a steak dinner."

"I only want to talk. You can bring your old Aunt Fanny as chaperone."

"I don't have an Aunt Fanny."

"That's OK, I'll bring mine. What do you say? A nice quiet meal at the Blue Ox."

That got her attention. "The Blue Ox? For real? No, forget it. You're too old."

"I'll say. But I'll put my teeth in before dinner."

"No. Look at you. You're pudgy."

"Pudgy? I like it. That's as good as chubby, or chunky. The truth is, I'm only a little big-boned around the belly. Come on, be a sport. I've really been craving a great steak dinner the last couple of days. But all my friends, if you'll believe it, are vegetarians. I can't show up at a swank place like the Blue Ox by myself. Folks will think I've been stood up. What do you say?"

She took her doe-like eyes off her keyboard just long enough to burn a couple of holes through my face with them.

"We're talking eating steak, answering some questions about Mr. Ravencamp, and nothing else?"

"Sure. That's the program."

"Boy Scouts honor?"

"I never made it past Cub Scouts, but I took knitting lessons from my old den mother. What if I swear on a skein of yarn?"

She switched her attention back to her Olivetti. "Where would you be picking me up? Assuming I'm going."

"Anywhere you tell me. Here at the office. At your Aunt Fanny's. Or we could meet at the restaurant."

She gave me a withering, unbelieving look.

"Meet you at the restaurant? Like I'm a bimbo?"

"OK. Give me an address. I'll be there at six."

"Don't wear that shirt. What'd you have for lunch? Eggs?"

The girl was a mind reader. She gave me a downtown address and told me to make it six-thirty. I agreed, and left.

Once outside I realized I'd forgotten something. I stuck my head back in the door.

"What's your name?" I asked.

"Carmen"

"As in Miranda?"

"Yeah. But I don't wear the hats. I'm ordering the T-bone. You OK with that?"

"Sure. You couldn't make me happier."

By the time I was back on the highway I was in a pretty good mood. I wondered why since I'd be emptying out my modest bank account to pay for two steak dinners at the unpretentious but costly Blue Ox. I'd probably have to shave again, and maybe even change my socks. As for my shirt, since Carmen didn't like it, I'd have to pull my other one from the clothes hamper and shake out the wrinkles. I might even have to fire up my iron.

I took stock of what I'd done so far. Nothing. All I'd learned at this point was that Roscoe Ravencamp was likely dead, but not by suicide or murder. And it was doubtful that he was still alive and had faked his own death. All my suspicions had proved likely but impossible to prove. Great. I decided to crawl back to my office and make some phone calls. It was two o'clock. I had plenty of time to waste before my dinner engagement.

When I unlocked and entered my office I was relieved to see that no one had broken in and cleaned the place while I was gone. Every cobweb and dust mote was still in place. Up in the corner of the ceiling, the dusty spider web with the dead spider and the dead fly — which had died first? — had not been desecrated.

Someday I'll get a real office, in a swank neighborhood. That's what I keep telling myself. For now, I'm stuck renting space in a building erected at about the same time as the Pyramid of the Moon in Mexico City. The only good thing about my office is that it's on the ground floor. My potential clients don't have to feel their way up the eternally dark stairwells.

The landlord changes out dead light bulbs as often as he has the windows washed, once every other leap year. The only alternative to the dim stairway is an elevator that shakes and jerks and occasionally pauses between floors to rest. The white-haired elevator boy — he's only sixteen — does a good business selling rosaries to his frightened passengers.

I almost missed seeing the folded sheet of paper torn from a spiral notebook that someone had shoved under my door. In fact, I didn't see it until I stepped on it and it slid out from under my shoe.

I went behind my desk and sat down before reading the note. You just never know what kind of news you're going to receive.

It turned out to be a missive, in terrible handwriting, from Rita Ravencamp's brother-in-law, Alvin. The note said he'd dropped by earlier but I hadn't been in my office. He said he'd try me again around three. There was a phone number for his locksmith's shop I could call if I wanted to talk to him before then. It was two-forty-five. I had time for a couple of phone calls before Mr. Ravencamp was due to arrive. I picked up the phone and called the Blue Ox to make reservations. Fortunately, they still had a table for two, right near the public bathrooms, which I thought was pretty handy.

At a few minutes before three, my investigative ruminations were disturbed by someone scratching at my office door. I opened it and a guy shuffled in and I guided him to the client's chair. He was forty or so, a little thick around the middle, with some dark hair plastered down to hide a bald spot. He was wearing a light jacket and a tie, but the latter was loosened and there was sweat fairly dripping off the guy's red face.

"Let me take your coat," I offered, before I sat down. "It's a hot one out there and it's none too cool in here."

He gratefully shed his plaid sports coat and I hung it up on the impressive hat and coat rack I'd bought at a junkyard to class up the place.

'I'm Alvin Ravencamp," he croaked, as soon as I'd sat down.

Up close he had a faintly medicinal smell. Whiskey, Kentucky, possibly rye. And not top shelf stuff. He wasn't drunk by any means, but he had a bloodshot, agonized aura. Really bad hangover, I diagnosed. Before speaking again, he pulled a linty handkerchief from a back pocket and swabbed his face with it. The hair that'd been covering his bald spot was sticking out all over now.

"I think you could use a drink," I said.

He nodded his head in agreement, and fished out a half-pint bottle half full of amber liquid from his hip pocket. He eyed it with a combination of fondness and regret, uncorked it, and politely offered me a swig. I declined, so he took mine for me before taking one for himself.

"Actually," I told him, "I was thinking a drink of water might do you good. You aren't used to hitting the pickle juice this hard, are you?"

"No. And I don't want you thinking I'm some kind of lush or something. But things have been tough lately."

"So I heard, from your sister-in-law."

"Yeah. Rita's taking it better than me. You know, when my brother disappeared a couple of years ago, I was a mess. Heebie jeebies like you wouldn't believe. And now that he's showed up, I'm a mess again."

He took another swallow of hooch, but the stuff

wasn't doing him any good.

"Nice cold water," I said, "and lots of it. That's what you need. Come on, allow me to lead you to the fountain of youth."

I took him out into the hall, and we navigated a few yards of ugly linoleum and around a corner to a frosted glass door that had "Vosscoff Enterprises" stenciled on it. As far as I could tell, the entire company consisted of crabby old man Vosscoff and his comely but vacuous daughter, Clementine.

I don't know what their real racket might have been, but when pressed, old Vosscoff claimed he made his living repairing dentures and glass eyes. I doubted if his real income was derived from any such innocuous or improbable enterprise, but it was really none of my business. I only stopped by Vosscoff Enterprises when I wanted to imbibe from their water cooler, or to cheer my spirits with a long look at Clem.

I rapped on the door and a small voice from inside beckoned us to enter. We went in, closing the door behind us.

"Busy?" I asked Clem, who was sitting at her desk doing nothing but her nails, which she was painting some color of pink.

"Not so much. How's it going, Slugger? It's been awhile."

"Too long. Say, would you mind if my friend here borrowed a couple of glasses of your excellent water?"

"Surely. Help yourself."

She smiled and I smiled back. I looked deeply into her cornflower blue eyes. There was no spark of sentience in them. They might as well have been doll's eyes.

I took a cone-shaped paper cup from the holder, filled it with cool water, and handed it to Alvin. He drank it down and I filled the cup again. He drank it down. I filled it again. He drank it down. You get the idea.

After he'd emptied about half of the cooler's water, I looked at Clem and saw her mouth hanging open. I leaned over her desk and whispered. "You'll have to excuse my friend. He just finished a hitch with the French Foreign Legion, and he's got kind of an emotional thirst."

"Sure, poor guy. He's welcome to as much water as he wants. The French Foreign Legion. Wow. I saw a movie about them. What's-his-name was in it. You know, the guy with the mustache?"

"Yeah. It's on his upper lip? I know the guy. He's an actor."

"That's the one. You saw the movie too? I liked those funny hats they wear, with the veils on the back. But all that sand! Is France really nothing but sand?"

"I'm afraid that's the case."

"I could never live there. I don't even like sand in my shoes. You couldn't get this girl to live in France if you were to put me up in the swankiest room in the Eye Full Tower."

I resisted an urge to pat her on the head. By now Alvin had slaked his enormous thirst. I slid a quarter across Clem's desk.

"For the water," I explained. "See you, Clem."

"Sure, you're welcome. Jeez."

5

By the time we'd made it back to my office, Alvin had started to perk up.

"That was a great idea you had," he said. "Thanks."

"You might want to ease up on the tarantula juice for a spell. You need to have your wits about you right now. I've heard Rita's version of your brother's reappearance, but what's your take on it?"

"No different from Rita's, I'm sure."

"But you're the one who first spotted Roscoe. Right?"

"I'm the only one who's seen him. Three times."

"Tell me about it. Would you mind if I lit up a cigar? Can I offer you one?"

He made a face. "To tell you the truth, I'm feeling kind of queasy. I'd really appreciate it if you didn't smoke right now. I mean, it's your office and all, but — "

"No problem. I'll smoke later. Go on with your story."

"It's like this. I never gave up on Roscoe. I try to be a positive guy, and I think I am most of the time. If Roscoe had hit his head when his car hit the water, and drowned, then they would have found his body. Otherwise, if he'd been conscious, he would have swam to shore. That's the kind of guy he was. So where does that leave us? Nobody was ever found, therefore he didn't drown! If he swam to shore, and I know he did, then for some reason he couldn't or wouldn't show himself.

"Now, me and Rita, we had this theory, almost from the first. We couldn't think of any reason why Roscoe would run away. He had a good life. No reason to give it up. And if he had some kind of dangerous enemies, for whatever reason, he wouldn't have hid from them. He wasn't that kind of guy. So, what does that leave? Roscoe hid himself because he didn't know any better. Rita and me, we got the idea that Roscoe must have got smacked on the head with a rock or something, and it did something to his brain. Like amnesia or something. Now, listen to this — were you in the war?"

I nodded.

"So was I. So was Roscoe. He was some kind of sniper or something, in the islands. I don't know exactly what he did because he wouldn't ever talk about it. Not to me, not to Rita. OK, there's a lot of guys like that. I think Roscoe lost his memory, part of it anyway, in that car accident. And I think he believes he's still in the war, surrounded by enemies. Rita probably told you that Roscoe kept a forty-five, a pistol, in the glove box of his car. The same kind of gun he used in the war."

"She told me. And when the car was pulled from the river the pistol was gone."

"Exactly. Now doesn't that tell you something?"

"Sure, but what?"

"It tells you that he thought he'd need a gun. He wouldn't have risked drowning to take that pistol out of the glove box unless he thought someone was going to try to kill him. He lost his memory and thought he was back in the war."

"If he'd lost his memory, how'd he know the pistol even existed?"

Alvin shook his head impatiently. "I don't have all the answers. It'd take some kind of head doctor or something to explain things so they'd make sense. If you want, I'll tell you what it adds up to for me. Roscoe's alive, but he doesn't know who he is. Now that he's shown up again in Crystal Quarry, you have to wonder if he's getting his memory back."

"OK. I'm not going to argue with you about any of this. I promised Rita I'd take the whole matter seriously, and I'm going to. Let's get back to when you first saw Roscoe after his return to the living."

"It was about three or four weeks ago. You'd

think I'd remember the exact date, but I was pretty shook up. I work on Quarry street, just like you. The business goes back to my Grandpa's time. He was the first locksmith in the family. Built the building where we're still located. Ravencamp's Keys and Locks, a little south of here. I'm sure you know the place."

"Sure. I've seen it."

"At least twice a day I drive by this old building that used to be a small quilt factory or something. I pass it to and from work, and sometimes more often. It's not a factory anymore. There's a tailor shop on the first floor, and the tailor and his family live on the second floor.

"There's a third floor, and it used to be apartments, but there's nobody living there now. I think the building's kind of falling apart, and the owner doesn't want to spend the money to fix it up, so the third story is pretty much boarded up. I know all this because I've looked into the matter after seeing my brother standing at the entrance to an alley that runs along one side of the building. "

"How could your brother be living there if the place is locked up?"

Alvin grinned at me. He looked like a happy young boy. "You're forgetting what I just told you. My grandpa started our locksmith business, and passed it onto my dad. Roscoe and me could pick locks before we were ten years old. Jimmying locks might be part of what my brother still remembers."

"Could be. Finish your story."

"Like I said, I drive by that building all the time. On this particular day I happened to look over at the tailor's shop while I was passing it. A curtain on a third-floor window moved, and a face looked out. It was Roscoe's face. Older, battered, but still his face. I just about wrecked my car right then. I had to pull over and sit by the curb for a while. That first time, I couldn't really believe it was him. I thought my mind must be playing tricks on me, or maybe my eyes.

"When I finally got home there was no one to talk to except the cat. My wife was out of town, still is, visiting her sister in New Mexico. She's pretty much moved down there, to be truthful. Her sister's marriage isn't going well. That's what Della, my wife, says. But now she's moved our kids down there, and they're enrolled to go to school in Farmington.

"Della hasn't mentioned divorce to me, but what other reason could she have for moving away, taking our two kids, asking for a separate bank account? I don't know if she's found some other guy, or what. Maybe it's me. Maybe I did something. Della's not direct. Not with me, not with anyone. So, when I saw Roscoe that first time, the only person I could talk to about it was Rita. It rattled her. I wish I'd never told her."

"You didn't think she should know? About her own husband?"

"Of course I thought she should know. But, it's

been two years. Rita's not the kind of woman who can live by herself. Two years is a long time. I think she might be seeing somebody new. Can you blame her?"

"Not at all. How did she react to the news?"

Alvin snorted. He took the bottle from his hip pocket and made it a little closer to empty. "She didn't believe me. Like you. Like the cops. Nobody wants to believe it. But I gave Rita proof, and now she knows Roscoe's alive."

"What kind of proof? The photographs?"

"Sure. What else? After that first sighting I started carrying a camera around with me. Two weeks went by and I didn't get so much as a glimpse of Roscoe. I started hanging around the building on my lunch hour. After work. Before work. On Sundays."

He found his bottle again, took a good swig. "Two weeks went by and I got nothing. No sign of Roscoe. And then, bingo. One day I was walking by the front of the building and had just reached the alley that runs along one side. I looked in the alley and there he was, not ten feet away. He just stood there, staring at me. Then I remembered my camera and took his picture.

"I said, 'Hey, Roscoe, it's me, your brother Alvin.' But he ran down the alley away from me. Actually, he limped. Something was wrong with one of his legs. And I'd seen a scar on his forehead and one on his throat. He's had a hard time of it, poor guy. It makes my heart bleed."

"OK, that was the first picture you took. What about the second?"

"I took that one only a few days ago. I was coming home late from work. It was already getting dark. I parked across the street from the tailor's. The shop was already closed and there were lights in the windows on the second floor. I grabbed my camera out of the car and put on the flash attachment. Then I walked slowly all around the building.

"There were some trashcans in back, and as I passed them I thought I heard a noise. I didn't have a flashlight with me, so when I heard the noise again, this time louder, I held up the camera and clicked a picture. The flashbulb lit up a pretty big space, and there was Roscoe, standing by a trashcan with something in his hands. Then it was dark again and I couldn't see him. But I could hear him moving around in the dark.

"I called his name, twice. I think he hesitated a moment, then limped away. I'm pretty sure he knows his name."

"Why didn't you run after your brother when you saw him?"

"I didn't want to scare him. I thought he might run away for good."

"All right. At what point did you confide in Rita, and when did the two of you call in the police?"

"I told Rita the same night I took the first picture. I stopped by her house and showed her the picture. I've got one of those Polaroid Land cameras. I thought she was going to faint. You just can't argue with those photos. It was Roscoe for sure.

"She was all for calling the police right then, so we did. They asked us if we could drop by the station if we didn't mind, since a couple of their squad cars were in the shop and they didn't have any to spare. And that's what we did. We drove down to the station, we told our story, and we showed them the pictures. We hadn't come up with our idea about Roscoe having lost his memory yet and thinking maybe he was back in the war. I'm glad, because if we'd told any such story I really think they would have laughed at us.

"They wrote down our story, took our personal information, and asked to borrow one of the photos so they could show it around. I didn't want to give up either picture, so Rita gave the cops an old picture of Roscoe she'd been carrying in her purse.

"The cops said they'd get back to us, but they never did. And when Rita contacted them and asked how the search was going, the officer she spoke to acted like the whole thing was a waste of time. That's when Rita first came up with the notion of hiring a private detective. I guess you know the rest."

"Yeah, although Rita made it sound like the two of you did some investigating on your own."

"That's right. Then we went back to the police. They still treated us like kids spooked by a Halloween prank."

"What about the building where you took the pictures, where you think your brother might be camping out? Did you tell me you talked to the tailor? What about the landlord?"

"Sure, the landlord and the tailor. Both a couple of dim bulbs. The tailor's some kind of Bohunk, and all he talks about is how hard he and his family work. Like I care. He said he didn't know if anyone was living on the third floor. Too busy to notice, he said. And when he and his family aren't working, they're sleeping like logs because they work so hard during the day. I couldn't get anything out of that guy. The landlord was worse. He's a nut. Thinks I'm going to turn him over to a building inspector, or something. I asked to see the third floor, but he turned me down. I gave up on him."

"So you haven't seen the inside of those closed-up apartments?"

"No."

"You didn't think of picking the lock?"

"That'd be illegal."

"But you want me to do it? At least, that's what Rita suggested."

"Sure, but you can do it officially. It'd be part of your job."

"I'd have to get the crazy landlord to agree to it, to letting me in."

Alvin shrugged. "I figure you've got ways. You're a detective."

"Sure. I'll just use my silver tongue to charm the landlord into letting me see his derelict third floor."

"Whatever it takes. You do this stuff for a living."

"I'll do what I can. You got the guy's name? The landlord? His phone number?"

"Name's Francis Swan. I don't have his number on me, but it's in the book."

"Did you say 'Swan'? The guy's nuts."

"I just told you that. You know him?"

"We've crossed paths. Swan owns a few properties in Quartz Quarry, mostly on the wrong side of the tracks. He believes Hitler is still alive and is secretly poisoning America's fruit trees. And that's one of his more reasonable beliefs. There's no chance he's going to cooperate with anyone but the police. Do you know if the cops have checked the place out?"

Alvin shrugged again. It was a gesture I was beginning to find annoying.

"If they have, they haven't told me or Rita. Listen, I'm going to throw out an idea and you tell me what you think of it. OK?"

"Sure. Shoot me the pill."

"I'm thinking you and me could go over, you know, to the tailor's place, right in broad daylight. We can drive over in my car. It says 'Ravencamp's Locks And Keys' on the doors. We'll just go over there and park in back, like we're doing a job, you know? We'll go up the fire escape stairs and check out those old apartments. Nobody's going to pay any attention to us. The tailor's going to be busy working, and the landlord won't be in the picture at all. It's the perfect setup."

"Sure. The perfect setup if you want the two of us to end up wearing zebra stripes. All we need to get caught is for one bored old lady, or man, to look out their window and wonder what's going on. They'll call the cops, and you and me will be turning boulders into gravel for the next couple of years. Come up with a better plan."

"No, it's a good plan. If the cops show up, we basically tell them the truth. We tell them I've been hired to change the lock on the door because somebody's maybe been staying in the place. The cops aren't going to call the landlord to see if it's true. They're too lazy."

"You don't have much of an opinion of our stalwart constables, do you?"

"About the same as you, I bet."

"So, what about me? How do we explain me?"

"Same thing. We tell the truth. I tell the cops that I hired you to look into my brother's reappearance. I have reason to believe that Roscoe's been staying in the very apartments this landlord just hired me to change the lock on so I called you so you could come along and check the place out."

"You'd make a pretty good crook, wouldn't you?"

"Hey, I'm an honest guy. Locksmiths have to be extra honest. I'm just good at figuring things out, that's all. Come on, what do you say? We can go right now."

"Let me think about it."

"There's no time for that."

"Maybe I think faster than some people. Give me a minute."

I knew I was going to give in, even though that nasty little brat inside my head was throwing a tantrum. Alvin had all the answers, I had to give him that. And this might really be the only way I was going to get inside the place. As usual, my curiosity got the best of me. I stood up.

"OK," I said, "let's go." I took my hat off the rack, and handed Alvin his jacket. "You got any mints to chew or anything? I don't think the cops are going to like your breath."

He reached into his pocket and brought out a handful of cloves.

"Want some? They really work."

"No thanks. I'm not the one that's been guzzling the saddle varnish. Let's get out of here and find your car."

6

Alvin's ride was an aqua Studebaker Champion, a nice little boat. Sure enough, 'Ravencamp's Keys and Locks' was painted on the two doors in white letters. He started up the fliver and we headed south a few blocks, then he passed a derelict brick building with a green canvas awning on the first floor. There were big letters on the awning that said, "Kremp's Fine Tailoring Mending & Altercations." I figured Alvin must be right about the tailor being a foreigner.

Alvin swerved the little Champion down a narrow alley and found a place to park behind the building. His driving wasn't too bad considering what he'd been having for lunch.

"This is perfect," he said, getting out of the car the same time as me and looking around. "Nobody's in sight but an alley cat. Let me get my tools."

He grabbed a red toolbox from the trunk and we headed up the wooden fire escape. About halfway up I realized I wasn't in quite the shape I'd like to be in. Alvin wasn't doing any better, and we were both huffing and puffing by the time we reached the third floor landing. There were some empty paint cans stacked on the second story landing but no other signs of civilization.

"Quite a view," said Alvin, looking out from the top of the stairs and leaning on the railing. He was lying. There was nothing to see but other brick buildings as ugly as our own.

"Try the door," he told me, "maybe I won't have to get out my tools."

I jiggled the doorknob. No dice, it was locked.

Alvin took a look. "Brand new lock. Must have scared the landlord when I called him. This makes it easy. If the cops show up I can show them that I just installed a new lock. It's like it was meant to happen."

"Let's not get carried away. I don't think it's time to contact the Vatican and tell them about the newest miracle."

Ignoring me, he bent over his opened tool box and selected a couple of picks and a small, flat bar, then went to work on the lock. It didn't take him long. Soon the door was unlocked and swinging open.

"I don't suppose you'd teach me how to do that, would you?" I asked him." You could make it part of my payment."

"No. You might get in trouble later on and I'd feel bad. Besides, I've got all the competition I need already."

We entered the dark, hot, musty interior of the closed-up apartments. The first thing I noticed was a hallway running the length of the building. There were four doors set into the wall facing us. A single window at each end gave the hallway a little bit of light, and you could see the dust motes hanging in the still air. A couple of bare bulbs would have lit the place further, but when I hit the switch on the wall next to the outside door, nothing happened

I tried the first door I came to. It opened. Inside was a dingy two-room apartment. An old rug covered most of the floor of the front room. This was obviously intended to be the living room, except for one corner that featured a counter and shelves, with enough space for a hotplate or toaster.

There was no running water. The second room was reached through a wide doorway with no door. It had one window at the far end that looked out on the street in front of the building. The place showed no signs of having been lived in anytime recently. Alvin and I looked at each other and shrugged.

We went out into the hall and tried the next door. It also opened. It looked the same as the first apartment, only shabbier. We tried the third door in the hall. It opened into a large bathroom with a chipped clawfoot tub, a large sink, and a stained toilet. The bathroom had apparently been shared by the dwellers of all the apartments.

At the back of this bathroom was a door that was locked. Alvin quickly jimmied it, but it wasn't worth the effort. It was only some kind of small storeroom, now empty. We went on to the fourth and last door opening off the hallway. There was nothing in this one either that would suggest recent visitors. If Roscoe, or whoever he was, had been living here, he had sure cleaned up after himself. I admit I felt a bit let down.

"Perhaps you were wrong," I told Alvin, who looked about as crestfallen as I felt. "Let's get out of here."

We were on our way down the hall when I thought of something. Why I hadn't thought of it sooner I can't say. "Wait a minute," I said to Alvin, "do you have a flashlight in that magic toolbox of yours?"

"Of course. Why?"

"The only door inside this place that was locked was the one leading off the bathroom to that storage area. "It was too dark in there to see much. Let's go back again and inspect the place with your flashlight."

"I think you might have something there. At least it's worth a shot."

"We'll need to hurry, though. If the police show up now there's no way you're going to convince them you came here just to replace the lock on that outside door."

"Don't bet on it. I think pretty well on my feet.

But we won't take any longer than we have to. Lead on, shamus."

I led on. We went back into the bathroom. Alvin had relocked the door when we left the first time so nobody would know we'd been there. Now he had to pick the lock again. He dug out a three-cell flashlight and we reexamined the storeroom. With the light we could see all kinds of evidence that somebody had been living, or at least sleeping, here.

There was a pile of worn blankets in one corner that had clearly been used as a bed. There was a partly burned-down candle stuck to a saucer, with a half-full box of candles nearby. There was a scotch bottle with about an inch of hooch left in it. And there was an empty coffee can with some sand in the bottom, and in the sand were some burned matches and the stubs of several cigars.

The bare floor was dusty in spots from where plaster had fallen down from the ceiling. It'd been walked on and the footprints were pretty interesting. Alvin was getting all excited.

"Roscoe's been here all right, no question of it. What did I tell you?"

"Never mind what you told me. Tell me instead how you're sure it's your brother whose been staying here. He isn't likely the only person in this town who's been wandering around without a home."

"It's obvious. There's evidence all over. The cigar butts. The bands show they're the same brand my brother smoked. And that scotch, that's not a common brand. It's the kind Roscoe always drank. But more than anything it's the footprints. Take a look at them. Here, I'll show you." He took me over to where the clearest set of prints were and shined the flashlight on them.

"Roscoe was an average-sized guy, like me, but his feet were small, like mine. These prints are small, but that's not what I wanted to show you. See, Roscoe broke his leg when he was just a kid. I pushed him out of a tree house, but never mind that. It healed fine, he never walked with a limp or anything, and it sure didn't keep him out of the army. But one of his feet was kind of crooked after the accident. His left foot sort of leaned in, so that part of his shoe sole wore down faster than the rest. See, look at these prints. There's a whole bunch of them here, so you can get a good look."

I looked. I followed the path of prints and, sure enough, the left ones had that funny pattern Alvin had pointed out. I was beginning to feel a little like Dr. Watson.

"All right," I told him, "you've convinced me. So what am I supposed to do about it?"

"I thought this was what you were looking for. Ain't that why we came up here?"

"I guess that's so, but I haven't given much thought to the next move. As I understand it, the way Rita presented it to me, I'm to gather evidence of your brother's being alive and possibly injured in such a way that he doesn't know who he is. Or even where he is. I'm to convince the cops that what you and Rita have been telling them is the straight dope. Either that, or I'm supposed to round up Roscoe all on my own and capture him, or whatever you want to call it. Is that about how you see it?"

Alvin was nodding even before I finished talking. "That's exactly right, Hatchett. So which do you want to do? Take more pictures of him and collect more evidence, or reel him in for me and Rita to take care of?"

"I'm not taking him in by myself. Can I count on your help?"

"No, I don't think so. I'd feel kind of funny about it. "

"So go ahead and feel funny, to your heart's content. I need your help. Yours or somebody's."

Alvin hemmed and hawed, and played with the flashlight. "Listen, I'll tell you the real reason I don't want to help you, OK? But you have to promise not to laugh, or tell anybody about it. Deal?"

"Yeah, sure. I'll put a lid on my laughter, and I won't give away your little secret to anybody. Will that work for you?"

"Promise."

"Cut it out. All right, I promise, cross my heart, spit on my grandmother's grave, the whole nine yards. Now spill it."

"See, it's like this. Della thinks I might be stepping out on her. My marriage is on the rocks, buddy. I'm scared. I'm not just afraid of divorce, I'm afraid of alimony and child support. Della and I are likely finished, but I still want to see my kids, and I don't want to be paying through the nose for the rest of my life because Della hired some shyster lawyer to milk me dry. She's got this idea, I think, of hiring somebody like you to follow me around and spy on me. If I was caught having an affair it could ruin me in the divorce courts. I'm trying to show her I'm innocent.

"I came up with the idea of having her call me at home at nights, all kinds of different hours, just to make sure I'm where I'm supposed to be. Della's friends with our nosey neighbors, and I'm sure they'd tell her if I was having any floozies over. God help me the one night I don't answer my phone at home. I couldn't ever reason with her, that's not Della's style."

"Why don't you let her go ahead and hire a detective to tail you, look into your private life, and find out what you're up to? It can't hurt you any if you're innocent. But maybe you aren't. Is that what you're saying?"

He turned a fairly bright red.

"A guy gets lonely sometimes. Like I said, my marriage is over. Maybe I've got things to cover up, but that ain't any of your damned business."

"All I'm getting out of what you're saying is that you can't help me on the stakeout."

"I'm sorry. That's how it's got to be. You married?"

"Don't even suggest such a thing."

"Someday maybe you will be. Just don't pick out a looker. That's what I did. Pick some nice amiable girl. Do you know anybody else who could help you with Roscoe? I thought private investigators had helpers. What do you call them? Operatives?"

"All of mine are working on other cases," I lied. "But I'll see what I can do. I sure don't want to go it alone, especially if your brother's packing a forty-five. What if he tries to use it on me?"

"Come on, Hatchett. You've got a gun, don't you?"

"More than one, but I don't like shooting them at folks. Guns get dirty when you fire them, and I don't like cleaning the things."

"Under no circumstances do you shoot my brother! You can fire a warning shot or two if you have to. What's the point of killing a guy who's just come back from the dead? Listen, if Della calls early enough, I'll come down and help you. What time do you think you'll be here?"

"I don't know. Obviously after dark. Don't worry about meeting me here. You might just screw things up if you show up later. I'll give you a call. What about the outside door? Any chance you can make me a key and drop it by my office?"

"No, not that lock. I'd have to pull it and take it back to the shop. You don't want that. Somebody might come snooping around here. "

"Then teach me how to pick it."

He shook his head. "No. Even if I wanted to, I couldn't teach you that fast. We'll just leave the door unlocked and hope for the best."

"Swell. "

"You'll be fine, don't worry. That lock on the outside door is a deadbolt. Just lock it from the inside when you get here. That way Roscoe won't suspect anything when he comes back."

"OK. Listen, I've got to get back to my office. You can drop me off there."

We left the way we came in, and in a few minutes I was back at my office. I figured I had plenty of time to head home, take a shower, grab my other shirt, and pick up Carmen for our heavy, or at least expensive, date at the Blue Ox.

I didn't have anything to do in my office. I'd just used that excuse to get Alvin moving. I locked up and retrieved the Hornet from its back-alley alcove. On the drive home I tried not to think about the Ravencamp case at all. I'd have plenty of extra time to go over what I'd found out later that night while I was on stakeout. Right now I contented myself by thinking of nothing at all.

7

I live on the west edge of town, which I guess has not grown much over the years. It's quiet, sparsely populated, with lots of mature trees, and even some brick sidewalks. What keeps it from being the high-rent district is the houses themselves. They tend to be pretty old and pretty small, and not especially comfortable. But definitely picturesque, as are the denizens who dwell there.

I inhabit one of a row of five little fake log cabins that crouch by the side of a gravel road. They were motel units until just recently, but they were falling into neglect and disrepair, and the owner sold them all off for a song. The enterprising individual who bought them started renting them out to childless eccentrics like myself who didn't need a whole lot of space, but who didn't favor apartment house living.

I liked living in a log cabin. It made me feel like Abe Lincoln, but without the beard or silly hat. I parked the Hornet in the front yard, unlocked the place, and walked into my living room, which is also the dining room. In one corner is a kitchenette where a resourceful bachelor like myself can hand craft toast, or boil coffee. Behind a curtained doorway is my bedroom, complete with a bed, a cedar-lined closet, and a window. There's also a bathroom the size of a phone booth, with a sink, a toilet, and a shower stall big enough for some adults. Mine is a life of unimagined luxury.

I pulled my extra shirt from the clothes hamper and hung it up in the bathroom while I took my second shower of the day. I shaved for the second time too, and rubbed some goo into my hair that made it stiff and bristly. I thought it looked pretty good.

The shirt was still a little wrinkled, so I stretched it out between the mattress and box spring of my bed, and took a short nap on top of it. That did the trick. I donned the shirt, added cufflinks, and my favorite tie, a pink silk number featuring a hand-painted trout whose dexter eye is made from a shiny and genuine sequin. I felt like it was prom night all over again.

It looked like rain, so I put the top up on the Hornet before I drove over to pick up the close-to-divine Carmen. I found her address OK, a small, roofed box that might grow up to be a house someday. She wasn't exactly waiting at the curb, but she came out the front door before I even had to honk. She had changed clothes and was wearing something on her head that she must have mistaken for a hat. When she was almost to the curb, she stopped in her high-heeled tracks and gave me a withering glare through the Hornet's passenger window. I got the hint and got out and came around and opened the door for her, and even closed it once she was inside.

"Nice tie," she said, when I was once again behind the wheel, but she didn't sound like she meant it. "Did you win it in some fishing tournament?"

"No. I'm not much of a fisherman. You look good. I love the hat."

We didn't say much more until we got to the restaurant.

Once inside the Blue Ox, we were greeted by roasted meat smells and a guy in a suit who wanted to know if we had reservations. He led us to a table with a top the size of a manhole cover, with a candle burning on it. Just as promised, the restrooms were only a few feet away. In less than a day, a waitress showed up and asked for our drink orders. I asked for coffee, and told Carmen to order whatever she wanted.

"You trying to make me drunk?" she asked, defiantly.

"No, I just want you to enjoy yourself. "

"I could drink you under the table."

"Sure, especially this table. Get whatever you want."

She turned to the waitress. "Bring me a boiler maker. Please."

The waitress disappeared and Carmen and I stared at each other over the candle flame.

"I'm not even sure I should be here," she said, finally.

"Of course you should. Are you kidding? There's a big juicy steak in the kitchen with your name on it. Which is better than having a cow with your name on it."

"Has anyone ever told you how charming you are? If I didn't believe you were as harmless as a puppy I wouldn't have agreed to go to dinner with you."

"Harmless? That hurts."

We read our menus — they were oversized, almost as big as the prices on them — until the waitress showed up with our drinks. After downing her shot of whiskey, and chasing it with half her glass of beer, Carmen became a little less venomous.

We both ordered fat steaks with all the trimmings, and when they arrived we ate in silence except for the gnashing of our teeth and the clashing of our cutlery. When our plates were clean, we pushed back our chairs and contemplated dessert. I figured it was time for Carmen to earn her dinner by telling me what she knew about her former boss, Roscoe Ravencamp.

"The trouble with bosses," I told her, "is that you have to work for them."

"You can say that again. I guess you don't have a boss, right? Must be nice."

"Anybody who hires me is my boss. But at least I get some variety. Why didn't Mr. Roman get a new partner when Mr. Ravencamp died?"

"I'm sure he doesn't want to share his profits. He has a bunch of underlings doing the work Mr. Ravencamp did. Also, we're not as busy as we used to be. And I wouldn't be surprised if Mr. Roman sold the company at some point. He's not much of a worker. I think all he brought to the partnership was some money, most of which he inherited. Things were sure different when Roscoe was still alive."

"You called him Roscoe?"

"You trying to say something? He asked all of us to call him by his first name. He was a dynamo. He did most of the work. At the time he died he was working on some deal that included his brother. I think Roscoe — Mr. Ravencamp — was counting on making a killing, but I actually heard that from his brother."

"Alvin? You knew Alvin?"

"Sure. He used to come into the office with his brother and kind of flirt with me. I think he missed his wife. She was away a lot."

"Even back then? She was visiting her sister, right?"

"That's what I heard. Alvin didn't talk about his wife much. He talked about the big housing development he and Roscoe were working on. I think their parents left them a big piece of land with orchards, and a lake, and I don't know what all. "

"How did the parents die?"

"Roscoe and Alvin's dad was killed in a hunting accident and their mom killed herself, so I hear. I never asked a lot of questions, you know?"

"Sure. Dessert?"

"Can I have whatever I want?"

"If it's on the menu, sure. Have another drink if you want."

I caught the waitress's attention by waving my napkin like a toreador, and both Carmen and I ordered dessert. She got the double fudge ice cream sundae, and I had rhubarb pie with a slice of Roquefort cheese and butterscotch sauce on top, and more coffee. I couldn't believe they charged me extra for the cheese.

"So," I said, when Carmen had started working her way through her sundae, "what happened to the big housing project when Roscoe died? I mean, did Alvin and Roman pursue it?"

Carmen stirred her ice cream and stared at the result as if reading tea leaves. "No. When Roscoe died, Alvin gave up the whole project. He did more than that. He sold the property to Rita, Roscoe's widow, for a dollar. That was nice, huh?"

I digested this information while I attempted to digest my dessert. "Interesting," I said, stirring my coffee, even though I take it black. "This piece of land, with its lake and all, it went to Alvin? What did Roscoe get?"

"Roscoe was left all the town property, including a big house and a couple of valuable vacant lots. You know, just looking at your dessert is making me sick."

"Look at your own dessert. So, when Roscoe died, Alvin sold his inheritance from his parents to his sister-in-law for a dollar. Kind of curious. You think maybe Alvin might have a yen for Rita? You think maybe that's what's really going on with Alvin and his absentee wife?"

Carmen started laughing, dribbling chopped nuts out of her open mouth. "You've met Rita, right?" she asked.

"I certainly have."

"But not Della, Alvin's wife?"

"No."

"They could be twins. Della's not a real red-head, but other than that, there's not much difference between them. Why would Alvin give up Della for Rita? What would be the point?"

"Well, first of all," I said, starting to get mad, "it sounds like Della's already left Alvin, and maybe Rita's got a personality more compatible with Alvin's. Have you thought of that?"

Carmen snorted derisively, "You're telling me that guys care about more than a girl's looks? You got any proof?"

I was taken aback. What a crass young lady Carmen was. "Well, I, for one," I told her, "look at things other than a trim figure and a pretty face. Personality matters to me."

"Sure, but that's you. What choice do you have?

A guy like you has to settle for personality over looks."

I flagged down our waitress again and asked for the check. When it arrived I took a gander and decided if I wrote a check for the full amount, plus the tip, I'd be able to cover it as long as I made it to the pawn shop before noon tomorrow.

When it came to driving Carmen back to her house, I was so full of new thoughts about the Ravencamp case that I could hardly even make small talk with her. She didn't seem to notice. When I pulled up in front of her house, she declined my offer to walk her to the door, and thrust her hand out to shake before I could even imagine such a thing as a goodnight kiss.

"Thanks for your help," I told her, as I helped her out of the Hornet, "and for the dinner company."

"It was a good steak," she allowed. "Don't be too hard on Alvin."

I took that home with me. Don't be too hard on Alvin? What the hell?

8

I had my camera in my car, and there wasn't anything else I needed before heading over to my stakeout at Roscoe's digs. I had my Chiefs thirty-eight special stuffed into my waistband, and I hoped I wouldn't need it.

When I'd told Rita I loved stakeouts, that they were like camping, I'd been lying. There is nothing worse, more boring, or generally more useless, than a stakeout. But it's often part of my job, and a paycheck is a hard thing to turn down.

However, on a stakeout you can't smoke — the smell, the glow of the coal — and you can't drink — you need all your wits. You can't even bring a thermos of coffee unless a toilet's right handy. No radio. No book or magazine because you can't chance a light for reading by. And you better not move around much because the wrong person might hear you. Of course, sleeping is out of the question; even nodding off for a minute. You've got to pay attention, all the time, even though there's nothing to pay attention to for most of your vigil.

I had a friend once, recently deceased, a shamus like me, who told me about going bear hunting with his dad each fall when he was a kid. They'd hike into the woods, and the dad would bring along some ripe carcass he'd found on the road on their drive in. He'd stake the carcass — skunk, raccoon, billy goat, or whatever — in a clearing in the forest. Then he and his kid, my friend, would climb up a tree, camouflage themselves with fresh-cut pine boughs, and wait. They'd stay silent and motionless for hours, keeping an eye on the offal they were using for bait. In good years, a bear would show up and they'd get to shoot it. Other years, no bear would show up. My friend told me that's what stakeouts reminded him of.

Of course, in the detective business you don't see any bears, you don't spend time with a rotting carcass, and there's more variety. You might catch a timid husband cheating on his wife, or a gardener burying stolen goods in his employer's garden to be recovered and sold later. A wayward daughter's wrong-headed boyfriend might make an appearance, or maybe a blackmailer or murderer might show up.

Tonight, a dead-man-come-back-to-life might be my reward for a patient vigil. Or an imposter, with a mask, pretending to be the late Roscoe for whatever reason. Or, perhaps, somebody determined to kill poor old Axel Hatchett for unknown reasons, or no reason. I might sit in the dark for hours, getting stiff and cranky, fear being my only relief from boredom. What a way to make a living.

There wasn't going to be much of a moon to-night, which I thought was a good thing. I arrived at the stakeout about nine. I was hoping I wasn't too late, but there was no way of knowing. If Roscoe was already back in his lair, he would likely be suspicious after finding the outside door un-locked. In that case I might as well go home and come back on another day. I was already regret-ting that I'd wasted time on a steak and a date and couldn't get to the apartment building earlier. I could only console myself with the thought that Carmen had given me information that would help me solve this case.

I parked my car down the street a ways and walked the rest of the way, then I spent a few minutes in the shadows before I approached the stairs that led to the apartments. Nothing stirred. I didn't see or hear anything, so I crept up the steps until I reached the third story. I tried the doorknob and was relieved that the door was still unlocked. That told me that it was unlikely that Roscoe had returned. Still, I entered the place with a good deal of caution.

I went through the whole place again as quietly as I could, covering the beam of my flashlight with my handkerchief to dim it, and keeping my re-volver in my hand. Nothing. There was no sign that anyone had been here since my last visit. The storeroom door off the communal bathroom was still unlocked. I considered holing up there to wait for the dead man, but even I'm not that big a chump. Instead, I went back to the outside door, and sat down in the hall near it. I got my camera ready, and I settled in to wait.

I'd been sitting on the floor for no more than a minute when I started cursing myself for not having stopped by my office to bring along the folding chair I keep there just in case I should have two clients in my office at the same time. But it was too late now. All I could do was hope Roscoe didn't stay out carousing too long, and that made me start thinking about his schedule.

It looked like he spent his daylight hours roaming the streets, and his nights sleeping, just like me. It didn't make sense. If he was trying to hide, and that's what Alvin and Rita believed, why wouldn't he sleep during the day and prowl the empty streets after dark? It was only a detail, really, but it was one more thing about this case that didn't add up.

Whether it was the heavy meal, or the boredom of having nothing to do, or both, I came very close to nodding off sometime during the next two hours. What kept me from it was the sound of someone picking the lock of the outside door I was drowsing next to. I barely had time to grab my camera and stand up before the door opened wide.

I pointed my Argus at the doorway and pressed

the shutter. The flashbulb went off and something made a roaring animal noise. Then the door slammed shut. For a second I wondered if the guy had come inside or gone back out. It only made sense that he would have run away. I found the door, opened it, and followed my quarry as best I could in the moonless dark.

I'd stupidly left my flashlight on the floor in the hall, but I still hurried down the steps as fast as I could. When I reached the second-story landing I crashed into something that made a lot of noise and knocked me off my feet. It was those damned paint cans I'd seen stacked in the corner of the landing earlier, only they weren't in the corner any longer. Somebody — who but Roscoe? — had moved them to form a sort of alarm for chumps like me to stumble into. I figured the idea was to warn Roscoe if someone tried to come upstairs when he was asleep. But the trap worked just fine with me going down the stairs. By the time I untangled myself from the paint cans and regained my feet, it was obvious I had no chance of catching up with Roscoe, limp or no limp.

All that noise of crashing paint cans, together with the bestial howl my visitor had let loose, was bound to wake somebody. The tailor, the neighbors, somebody. It wasn't the kind of neighborhood where folks generally called the cops, but you never know. I needed to clear out. All I'd left upstairs was my flashlight, and I decided to leave it. Nobody was going to check it for fingerprints or anything, and I didn't want to get caught in the apartments while I retrieved it. I'd add it to my expenses, and Rita and Alvin could pay for it.

I made my way back to my car, fired it up, and dug my spurs in. I needed to get home and get some sleep so I could get up early and visit Grant, my photographer friend, to develop my picture for me. In fact, I almost called Grant to tell him I was on my way over for a late-night development, but Grant can be irascible at the best of times. Then I wondered about calling Alvin, or Rita, and telling about what had just transpired, but I decided to wait until I got home before making that decision.

When I pulled into my front yard, my headlights revealed a pair of luminous eyes less than a foot from the ground and near my door. Ambrosia, my pet skunk. I don't let her into my house, but I put out scraps for her, and I let her sleep in my crawl space in the winter. I pretend she's a cat. Ambrosia got pretty close to me when I got out of the car.

"I know, you smell steak on my breath, don't you? I should have saved you some scraps, and I would have, but I was distracted. Come around later and I'll have some bacon for you."

My words had the hoped for pacifying effect, and Ambrosia ambled off into some nearby bushes, and I ambled off to my bed.

I woke up around seven. I made a pot of coffee, applied heat to a couple of eggs, and burned some bacon, making sure to set aside a couple of strips for Ambrosia. I was out the door by seven-thirty.

Grant's Snapshot Cottage — a silly name if I've ever heard one — was housed in such a small place that I don't know how Grant fit all his cameras and stock, plus his darkroom, into it. Grant himself was about the size of a cape buffalo. I parked in the alley and pounded on the back door where his darkroom was located. I kept pounding until the old buffalo opened the door

"You'll pay double," he growled, as he let me in. "How many rolls of film have you got?"

"Just one."

"And it can't wait for one more hour?"

"I'm busy. It's very important."

"And how many exposures?"

"One."

"One? You're going to waste an entire roll of film for one picture? Go take some more. Come back when you've finished the roll. "

"I'm in a hurry."

"Then take some shots of my shop. Or, better yet, let me take some nice portrait shots of you. For your mother."

"My mom knows what I look like, and she's none too happy about it. Come on, Grant, what do you care? I'll be paying you double for a whole roll of film and I'm only getting one picture. "

"I have to develop the whole roll anyway, pal, even if it's for one print."

"I want copies. Two or three if it turns out

good."

Grant shook his big head, a look of angry sorrow on his face. "One exposure," he said. "It's a crime. Give me half an hour."

"For one picture? All right, I'll wait."

"No you won't. I'm a sensitive artist, I don't need you hanging around. Go have breakfast and come back in thirty minutes. There's a diner, Rocko's Kitchen, a couple of blocks north of here. Everything they offer is horrible. You'll love it."

"I already had breakfast. I'll go for a walk and be back in twenty minutes."

"Half an hour. Scram."

I wandered around for a while, but somehow ended up in front of Rocko's. You could smell the stale grease through the closed door, and it kind of made me hungry. I went in and ordered coffee and a donut. The donut was yesterday's. So was the coffee. The gal at the counter was short and mean looking.

"Don't you serve anything fresh in this place?" I asked.

"Just you, sailor. You want fresh food, grow it yourself."

"I would, but my coffee crop isn't doing too well this year, and the squirrels have been eating the donuts straight off the tree."

"Grew up on a farm, huh?"

The filthy wet rag she was swabbing down the counter with came dangerously close to touching my donut.

"Watch it with that thing, will you? I haven't been vaccinated."

"Smart guy. You married?"

"Only to my job."

"Yeah? Hard worker, huh? Listen, you ever want to share some of that money you're making, come look me up."

"That's a swell idea." I threw some change on the counter and made my escape while she pounced on it. Close to half an hour had passed by the time I got back to Grant's. He had my picture ready.

"Just the one print?" I asked.

"You said you wanted copies if it turned out well. Does that look like a good picture to you?"

It didn't, but I liked it anyway. What I held in my hand was a slightly blurred photo, taken too close, of a guy with his mouth wide open and his arms stretched out. He looked scared and surprised, the way I'd felt when I took the picture. It was the same guy as in the pictures Rita had given me. Roscoe Ravencamp. He wore a hat and the same horn-rimmed glasses he'd had in the other photos. And clutched in his right hand was something anybody who'd been in the army would have recognized, a Colt forty-five automatic. I'd carried the same kind of pistol myself and knew how deadly it was.

"Why are you looking pale?" Grant asked me. I'd forgotten about him. "Is that a ghost you took a picture of?"

"No, but it looks like he almost made a ghost of me. I'm glad he decided to run from me instead. Listen, I want five prints of this picture. Save the negative. I'll be back later to pick them up. Here" I handed him half a sawbuck.

"That's too much."

"Give me my change when I get back. Thanks."

I walked out the door to my car, fired it up, and headed for my office. I had a couple of phone calls to make and some thinking to do, and what better place to do both than my office?

Rocko's donut was having a pretty serious argument with Rocko's coffee in my belly, so I was somewhat distracted when I called Rita. I don't know why I called her first instead of Alvin, but that's what I did. She didn't pick up until the eighth ring and she sounded tired.

"I didn't wake you up, did I?" I asked.

She answered in a suddenly wide-awake voice. "Hatchett, is that you? I'm afraid you did wake me up. But that's all right. I had a rough night of it. Couldn't fall asleep for some reason. I was thinking too much about your stakeout. I almost called you about three this morning, but I didn't even know if you'd be home. What happened?"

"I've got something to show you. Do you want to meet me at my office, in an hour or so?"

"I'll be at work by then. Why don't you drop by my shop in a little bit. Can you be there in an hour?"

"Sure. Give me directions."

I hung up and then called Alvin's shop, but no-body answered, so I tried him at home and got the same response I'd gotten when I called Rita: eight rings and a tired voice.

"What's going on, Alvin? Did you wait until your wife called last night and then go out on the town?"

"No such thing. And don't try to tell me you tried to reach me earlier, because I've been here the whole time and the phone hasn't rung once."

"Why so tired sounding?"

"Not tired, a little hung over is all. But this morning I tried that trick of drinking a lot of water like you showed me. And I got to admit, I feel better. Did you do your stakeout last night?"

"I sure did. And guess who showed up for a visit?"

I could hear him draw his breath in sharply.

"Roscoe! You didn't catch him, did you?"

"Not a chance, and it's a good thing I didn't try. Your brother brought his pet pistol with him. But I got lucky. When I fired a flashbulb in his face, he chose to run instead of shoot me. Otherwise, I wouldn't be around to call you."

"Look, I'm sorry, but you can't say you weren't warned."

"I wish you'd been there with me."

"You know I couldn't be there. This thing with Della is serious. Did you get any pictures?"

"I did. It was your brother all right. I called you to ask what my next move should be. Your brother is probably going to abandon that apartment after finding me there. I haven't any idea where he'll go next. Have you?"

"Another empty building, I'm guessing. Maybe you can set a trap for him."

"Using what for bait? Rita?"

"If he even remembers who she is."

"You said he recognized his name when you called out to him, so he remembers some things. Rita might be one of them. Still, you'd have to know where to set the trap. Any other ideas?"

"Naw. Rita's better with ideas than I am. Maybe you should talk to her."

"I'll be meeting her at her shop in a little while. Care to join us?"

"I'd like to, but I really can't. I've been doing a little too much drinking lately. I'm behind in my work at the shop."

"I'm beginning to think you don't like spending time with me, Alvin. But never mind, I'll catch up with you later."

9

Rita's Art and Such was strategically located on the edge of a fairly old and exclusive residential neighborhood known as Bentwood Bluffs. There weren't any bluffs anywhere near the area. Or bent wood, for that matter. But what the hell. The houses were few and far apart, with lots of trees and shrubbery, some of it wild, to ensure that no one had to get cozy with his neighbors unless he wanted to.

The art shop was housed in a rambling frame building that might have started out as a chicken coop. When I opened the front door a merry little chime sounded. I found myself in a lobby area with a large cement fountain cunningly contrived to counterfeit a pile of rocks with water leaking out of it. A framed painting covered one wall. It was one of those pictures that can only be appreciated at the proper distance. I was too close. Maybe half-a-mile too close.

While I was admiring the lobby, the sound of

light, feminine shoe heels approached from somewhere in back. In a moment Rita stepped through a curtained doorway and greeted me. She looked swell. Today she wore some kind of flimsy flowered dress, with pleats in the skirt and some sort of crossover arrangement up top that did nice things for her torso. The dress was yellow and it went well with her red hair, which was twisted up into a kind of sailor's knot behind her pretty neck.

"Why didn't you come on back?" she asked. "Were you waiting for me to come get you?"

"I was simply admiring the artwork in your lovely anteroom here, especially the painting. It's too bad the artist didn't have anything smaller than a coal shovel to paint with."

Rita laughed. A fairly musical sound. "If Milton were here he'd call you a philistine."

"Who's Milton, the guy who painted that thing?"

"No, but he is an artist, and an art instructor. He paints, sculpts, even does some photography. And he works for me part time. We've known each other for years. He's not always polite."

"Sounds like my kind of guy. But, speaking of photographs, I've got a pretty special one for you. I took it myself."

"I can't wait. Come into the shop with me."

I followed her into a big, low-ceilinged room. The first thing I noticed was that the inside of the shop was a lot less high-toney than the entry. There was a lot of pottery laid out on tables and on shelves against the wall. Paintings covered the walls, with some papier-mâché masks here and there. There was even a glass display case full of jewelry and knick-knacks. Some sculptures were arranged here and there, mostly in the way. As far as I could see, Rita and I were alone. She led me over behind a counter with a cash register on it and offered me my choice of barstool-like chairs.

"It's just the two of us, so you can say what you like," she said. "I don't want everyone to know about Roscoe's reappearance. When Alvin called and told me you were going to be on stakeout, I was worried. For you, and for my husband. You said you have a picture to show me. Let's start with that, shall we?"

For some reason I didn't feel quite ready to show her the photo or tell her my story. I smiled at her, and she smiled back. I walked over to one of the walls decorated with masks. There were a couple I recognized as the masks of Comedy and Tragedy. I looked at Rita over my shoulder.

"Look at these two," I said, pointing at the masks. "They're both looking at the same thing, whatever it is. You, maybe. But this one's laughing and his brother is starting to blubber. That's people for you."

"That's Roscoe and Alvin, you mean," Rita said, while I walked back and sat on the stool beside her. "We grew up together, went to the same schools. Alvin was always the happy-go-lucky clown, never worried about a thing. Roscoe was serious from the day he was born, I swear. He always considered life a hard nut to crack. He never played much, mostly just counted the coins from his allowance that he'd managed to save up. He almost never spent a cent. That's why I always went to Alvin when I wanted to have fun. I knew he would happily spend every cent he had on me. But if I wasn't around, he'd spend it on someone else.

"When Alvin got drafted, he asked me to marry him, but I turned him down. I wanted kids and a family. I wanted a husband who was steady, reliable, a good provider, and that wasn't Alvin. It was Roscoe. Roscoe knew what the score was, but he kept his distance until his own draft notice came. Then he asked me if I'd marry him when he got back. I was like a lot of girls back then. I thought it would be romantic to have a fiancé in the war. Someone to write me letters, send me silly little presents. Someone to worry about, and whose picture I could wear in a locket near my heart."

"Sure, and I'll bet Roscoe liked it just fine too. Having a pretty girl whose picture he could show to his fellow dogfaces. Somebody back home who'd already promised to marry him. Guys like that were the lucky ones."

"Were you in the war?"

"Yeah. I was the guy who won it."

She laughed. "Did you have a special girl waiting for you at home, Mr. Hatchett?"

"Of course. My mother. She used to save her sugar rations for me, to bake little cakes to send me. Not one of those little cakes made it through the mail in edible form. But, what the hell, Mom wasn't much of a baker anyhow."

"No, you're just being modest. You probably had lots of girls waiting for you."

"Never mind that. What happened to Roscoe in the war? He became a sniper, right?"

"Yes. He never talked much to me about it."

"How about laugh-a-minute, stop-me-if-you've-heard-this-one, Alvin? What'd he do in the war?"

"Collected a couple of ugly tattoos. Or so I've heard. He was an office clerk in Tulsa most of the time. And you? Lots of heroics?"

"Me? I was General Patton's personal potato peeler. And he was mighty picky about his spuds."

"Are you ever serious?"

"Always. Listen, let's get back to why I'm here. Let me show you a picture of your husband. It's a bit blurry, but I had a hard time getting him to pose."

I took the photo from my jacket pocket and handed it to her. She took it in one of her dainty hands, all playfulness gone from her features now.

"Do you believe me now?" she asked. "It's him, it's Roscoe. He looks scared."

"I imagine he was. He comes home from a long day of skulking, and some gumshoe pops a flashbulb in his face. Still, it looks like he might have been expecting trouble. He had his pistol handy."

"I'm sorry. I did warn you, but it was never my intention to put you in danger."

"Don't fret over it too much. You're right, you did warn me, and this is hardly the first time I've faced some mug with a gun in his hand. Anyhow, now that I have this picture, you think it might be time to go to the cops?"

She hesitated. "I'm not sure I'm ready for that. If the police see this picture of my husband with a gun in his hand, who knows what they might do? I mean, they could go from not believing us at all to starting a full-scale manhunt. I think you need to keep handling matters on your own for a while longer, if you don't mind. Of course you're getting paid for it."

"Of course."

"But if you're too afraid — I mean — there's nothing wrong with that."

"Of course not. Lots of grown men get scared, even private investigators. Just don't tell the other guys about the stuffed bunny rabbit I keep next to my pillow."

She gave me an annoyed look, and she did it well. "All I'm saying is, don't continue with the case if you don't want to. We can just tear up the contract and Alvin and I will hire someone else. Perhaps you could recommend someone."

"Not a chance. I don't believe in helping out my competitors. But I've got a big question for you.

What's my next step?"

"Continue tracking my husband. That was the idea all along, wasn't it?"

"Wait a minute," I said, starting to get a little heated. "Both you and Alvin wanted me to photograph your husband and have some kind of contact with him as early as possible. If you just wanted me to track him, I should have watched that apartment from my car and not made contact. I should have tailed him, not let him know I was there, and found out where he goes during the day.

"If I'd done that, Roscoe would still be sleeping above the tailor's shop every night and we'd know where we could get our hands on him. But you and Alvin were in a hurry, and now there's no way of knowing where Roscoe is. It'll take me a lot of work to track him down. Maybe you really do need to hire a different detective."

She listened to all this without saying a word. If she'd had a tail it would have been between her legs. I almost felt like a heel. Almost. And then she surprised the hell out of me by laughing. It was a lovely sound.

"Quite the fire breather, aren't you?"

"I like a cigar now and then, if that's what you mean."

"You're right. Alvin and I didn't think things through very well. But why didn't you insist on doing things your way?"

I shrugged. "The customer's always right. I try

to do what I get paid to do, but now we're back to square one. Don't worry, it may not take long. I've found many a missing person in my line. But when it comes to capturing the guy, I don't want to be alone. I'll need help, and I may need to call in the police."

"Fair enough, I guess. But I do hope you can keep the police out of it."

The chimes that I'd heard ring when I'd arrived sounded again, and a moment later a guy walked in looking like he was visiting his own hangman.

"Good morning, Rita," he said. He didn't speak to me, but gave me the kind of look most people reserve for rodents. The guy was medium height, middle-aged, with a pinkish complexion and quite a bit of sandy hair combed to perfection. He was dressed neatly, almost foppishly, in clothes that were well cut but by no means new. He looked like a fashion-plate hobo. He had a prissy manner that seemed to irritate even him.

"Good morning, Milton. I'd like you to meet Axel. He's doing a little work for me and Alvin."

Milton fastened his flinty doll's eyes on me for a moment, then reluctantly held out a soft white paw. I embraced it with my own somewhat coarser paw, but the gesture didn't make us friends for life.

"Rita tells me you're an artist," I said, smiling with as many of my teeth as I could.

"I've been called worse. And what line are you in?"

"Me? Oh, a little of this and that."

"Sounds lucrative." He glanced at Rita and said, "I've got some crates to unpack." He headed off to a back room somewhere, neglecting to tell me how nice it'd been to meet me. That was OK; I felt the same. I turned to Rita. "Listen, I've got to go. If you need anything, give me a call at my office. If I'm not there, try my home number."

Back out in the parking lot, I noticed what must have been Milton's car. It was a yellow Buick Roadmaster, not new, but in pristine condition. This guy wasn't well off, but it looked like he might have been a few years ago. However, since the guy wasn't part of the case, I put him out of my mind.

I stayed in my office only long enough to open and throw out my mail, then I drove back to Grant's, picked up my prints, and told him to hold the negative for me. It was lunchtime, but I wasn't hungry yet, so I decided I'd make a surprise visit to Alvin at his shop, hoping he'd be in. He'd given me his card, so I checked the address and rambled over there. It was a long, narrow, brick building painted an unnecessarily-bright salmon color.

When I opened the glazed front door, I got a bell instead of chimes. A sulky-looking kid of about twenty was standing behind the counter, near the cash register, staring at a collection of padlocks across from him. He turned toward me and showed a very sad smile.

"How can I help you?" he asked, sounding like

a funeral parlor employee.

"Is your boss in by any chance? Mr. Raven-camp?"

"Yes. Did you want to see him?"

"Yeah."

"He's in his office. I think he's on the phone. May I give him your name?"

"Axel Hatchett."

"Really?"

"Really."

He ambled piteously through a narrow aisle between safes of various sizes and colors. In a couple of minutes he was back.

"He's still on the phone, but he said for you to come on back. I'll show you."

I followed his hearse-like progress back to Alvin's office. Alvin, with a phone receiver stuck to his ear, was sitting behind a desk as sturdy as one of his safes. He smiled and motioned me to a chair in front of his desk. When he hung up he stood and reached over the desk to shake hands with me.

"I've been trying to reach you," he said. "Tried your office, tried your house. Finally I called Rita and she said you'd just left her place. I forgot you said you were going there."

"I've brought you a copy of the picture I took last night. It's not much, but at least we can prove that somebody besides you has seen the resurrected Roscoe. He caught me napping, I'm sorry to say, but I did get the one picture. I also tried to follow him down the steps, but he'd set a trap for me, a bunch of stacked-up paint cans. I about cartwheeled down the last flight of steps, and he was nowhere in sight when I hit the ground." I handed Alvin the picture. "You can see he had his gun handy. "

"I'm sorry I couldn't be there. Next time, I'll be there for you. I promise."

"Next time, huh? I don't know when that's going to be. Now that Roscoe's been tipped off, it might be pretty hard to track him down again."

"Yeah. Rita told me you're not too happy about the way things have gone. We're amateurs at this, me and Rita. What can I say?"

He reached into a desk drawer, drew out a pint bottle of something clear, gin or vodka maybe. He held the bottle up and raised an eyebrow at me.

"No thanks," I said. "Listen, it's none of my business, and since you own this place you can't be fired, but you might want to lay off that stuff when you're not at home."

"I know, I know. You're right. This is no kind of behavior for a business owner. But it calms my nerves, and I need that right now. I'll quit when all this crap with Roscoe is over. But I'm feeling better, thanks to you."

"How's that?"

He reached under his desk and brought forth a big metal thermos jug.

"Water," he said. "Nice cool water. You were right about that."

"Glad to be of service. You got any questions for me?"

He shook his head. "No, I guess not. Do you really think Roscoe might have shot you?"

"How would I know? He's your brother. I've got a question for you. What, exactly, do you want me to do? You and Rita are paying the tab, so what do you want your money to pay for?"

"Whatever you say. You're the doctor, so to speak. It sounds like me and Rita screwed up by not giving you more time. Well, now we're giving you the time. You take it from here."

I was disappointed. I'd been kept in the dark about a whole lot of things, and it was time to raise Alvin's hackles, if he had any. But first, I reached into my pocket and grasped my sap — a little leather cylinder stuffed with a couple of shotgun shells' worth of lead shot. I'd made it myself during one of those long winter evenings I sometimes have, for just this sort of occasion.

"Rita tells me you and her were quite an item before the war," I told him. "Roscoe got in the way. Then he died, and that gave you another chance with Rita. But with your brother coming back from the dead he's thrown a monkey wrench into your plans. It looks like Della wasn't the problem after all."

He was quick for a clumsy-looking guy with a skin full of hooch. Before I could do anything about it, he'd gotten out of his chair, reached across the desk, and grabbed a generous portion of my shirt collar in his fist. I drew the sap from my pocket and swung it down on the bony part of his exposed wrist. He yelped like a tail-stomped pooch and jumped back. When he grabbed the knob of the center drawer of his desk and started to pull it open, I dropped the sap and put my hand inside my jacket and shook my head. He stopped.

"Let's not either of us do something our Sunday school teachers wouldn't approve of," I warned.

He slammed the desk drawer shut and glowered at me with eyes that were more than a little bloodshot. For a moment, he looked almost as ugly as his brother.

"Get out of here," he barked. "You're fired, you lousy, nosey peeper."

"You might want to talk to Rita about that."

"Rita wants you gone already. I talked her into keeping you. But, guess what? I've had a change of heart. Now get out. I don't want to see your bulldog face again. Skedaddle."

I skedaddled, first retrieving my hat and sap from the floor where they'd fallen during our scuffle.

"If you change your mind," I told the still-simmering Alvin, "you're going to have to tell me a whole lot of things you haven't told me yet."

I backed out of the office and closed the door for him. On my way out, the junior undertaker at the cash register gave me a sorrowful nod.

10

I was glad it was over, I really was. It's not that I like being unemployed — and I was already regretting the expensive steak dinner with Carmen — but I just didn't like this particular case. My clients were keeping secrets from me, and that was both annoying and possibly dangerous. I'd find something else, and I'd go on with my rich and rewarding life.

But for now, at least for the moment, I felt the freedom that only someone playing hooky can feel. In fact, I was feeling so good I decided to go ahead and have a nice lunch instead of stopping at some miserable automat or lunch counter. I thought about what I really wanted to eat, and it came to me: a big, fat, greasy bratwurst, in a thick bun, smothered with a wheel-barrel load of sauerkraut. And I knew just the place: Karl's Kraut House.

Maybe I'd been thinking about it all day without knowing it. Karl's was over by Rita's Art and

Such, and I'd driven by it twice that morning without even noticing it, despite its being fairly noticeable — a bright yellow two-story house with red gingerbread trim and fancy fake shutters.

When you go inside you're greeted by a hundred or so quacking cuckoo clocks. The waitresses wear frilly white dresses with red aprons, thick red shoes, and improbable yellow wigs complete with braids. I could do without the polka-and-schnapps atmosphere, but I do like the food, even though it gives me gas. I was practically drooling at the thought of a bratwurst.

I parked next to a squarish maroon Ford and went inside the restaurant. It was about one-ten according to my watch, but about half the damn cuckoo clocks were chirping and warbling away like they had no idea they were supposed to tell the time. I seated myself at a table for two against a wall devoid of clocks.

I played with the salt and pepper shakers and the sugar dispenser until a waitress showed up. She was closer to four feet high than five, and I doubted she weighed much more than the clunky shoes she wore. She didn't really fit the image of the buxom beer-garden girl she was dressed to resemble, though her name tag declared she was named Heidi. All the girls in Karl's were named Heidi, or Helga, or Ingrid, or Ursula.

This particular Heidi tried to talk me into ordering a big foaming stein of beer, but I stuck with my usual coffee, and ordered two bratwursts buried under sauerkraut. While I was waiting for them, I took a gander at my fellow diners, a well-mixed lunch crowd. I heard a laugh I thought I recognized, and looked over at a table across the room from me. Seated together, at a table as small as mine, were Rita and Milton.

Though it'd been Rita's laugh that had caught my attention, she and Milton looked as if nothing in the whole world could be funny. A more solemn pair I hope never to see again. They appeared to be unaware of my presence, and I thought I might want to keep it that way. It was no great coincidence that the three of us should end up lunching at Karl's at the same time; the place was a handy spot for them.

I wondered if Alvin had managed to call Rita before she left her shop for lunch. If he had, any conversation I might have with her now could prove unpleasant. I decided to bury my face in my food, which had just arrived, and hope Rita didn't notice me.

I'll say this about Karl's, they didn't skimp on the food. By the time I'd gotten through both brats, and their burden of pickled cabbage, the German potato salad, and the dill pickle spears, I was ready to call it a day. I'd even managed to forget about Rita and Milton. But I didn't escape the restaurant unnoticed.

When I looked up from my empty plate, Rita was standing next to my table, smiling down at me as if I was the most wonderful man on earth, but I expect that's the way she treated most men. Her attentions could be very flattering, I must admit, but her smile on this occasion told me that she hadn't yet heard about Alvin's firing me. And, interestingly, Milton was nowhere to be seen. She must have sent him off to the parking lot so she could have a word with me in private. Or as private as a crowded restaurant can be.

"It's too bad I didn't spot you earlier," she said, or rather, crooned. "We could have had lunch together."

"Some other day, maybe."

"So, how have you spent the day since you left me? Do you have anything to tell me?"

"Sure. Your brother-in-law fired me about an hour ago. I thought maybe he would have called and told you."

She looked honestly shocked. "Alvin fired you? That's ridiculous. Why would he?"

"Well, I guess I riled him a little. You know, I haven't seen a whole lot of that happy-go-lucky side of Alvin you've told me about. He tried to pull a gun on me, and he wasn't laughing when he did it."

"Alvin? He doesn't even own a gun. As for his present behavior, you can imagine how upset he is these days, and I'm sure you know he's been drinking. But he's never violent. Tell me what happened."

"I just asked him a couple of questions. Maybe they weren't very nice questions, but I needed them answered. Digging up dirt is part of my job."

"What kind of dirt were you trying to dig up, Mr. Hatchett? You can tell me."

"I wanted to know if his brother's apparent death gave him any ideas of renewing his romantic attention's to Roscoe's comely widow."

A spot of angry scarlet lit up both of her cheeks for a moment, but when she spoke it was pure maple sugar. "I can understand why such an inquiry would upset Alvin, though I'm sure you meant no harm. Just look at the situation. Alvin's still married to Della, and even if the marriage goes south, I can't imagine him looking for a new wife before he's divorced. He simply isn't that way. He's an honorable man."

"Yeah, honorable and happy-go-lucky, and he doesn't keep a gun in his desk drawer at work."

"Believe whatever you want, but I'm telling you what I know. As for my being available, I'm not just anybody's widow. I'm Alvin's brother's widow. I'm sure he'd consider romancing me a form of poaching, no matter how dead Roscoe was, and I'm disappointed you didn't take my feelings into account. I would never allow Alvin to so much as look at me after I married Roscoe. And, finally, I'll never be able to view Alvin that way again. I got rid of any such notions years ago, before I married Roscoe. Does that satisfy your curiosity?"

"Not that it matters now. Not to me, anyway."

"In the first place, why did you want to know?"

"I was thinking about Roscoe. I was worried about you and Alvin. But never mind, it was just an idea, a long shot."

She smiled. "May I sit down?"

I scrambled to my feet and helped her into the adjacent chair. "Forgive my lack of manners," I said. "I was raised by carnival freaks. Would you like dessert? I'll pay, of course."

"No thanks, I've already had dessert. German chocolate cake. Very filling. But you go ahead."

I shook my head. When Heidi, or Hilda, or whoever it was, came by the table, I ordered more coffee and asked for the check. Rita leaned forward until her pointy breasts in her yellow dress almost touched the tabletop. She gave me an impish smile.

"Tell me about your silly idea. About worrying about me and Alvin."

"It's nothing much, but I thought perhaps Roscoe's showing up in town right now might have a purpose. I thought he might have returned because he got wind of his brother's interest in you, and vice versa. I thought he might have come back to put the fear of God into the two of you."

"You make it sound as if Roscoe had his full mental faculties, or as if you believed he arranged his accident so he could disappear."

"If he's still alive, that's the only thing that makes sense. I can't buy the idea of his wandering around with amnesia for two years. Why wouldn't he be spotted? How would he have made a living?"

"I'm sure you're wrong. Roscoe wouldn't have run away from me. As for Roscoe wanting to hurt me or Alvin, I can't believe that." She paused. "Listen, I've got to get back to the shop. When you finish your coffee can you give me a ride back? I had lunch with Milton, but when I saw you I sent him back to work in my car. Would that be all right?"

"Sure, just give me a second here."

I gulped down the rest of my coffee, left some change on the table for Hilda — or whoever — and headed for the cash register with Rita in tow. I lightened my wallet just a little, and we went outside to my faithful Hornet. Rita didn't like what convertibles did to her hair, so I put the top up. On the way to her shop I kept sneaking looks at her legs in their sheer stockings. She didn't talk any until I'd delivered her to her door, then she sat in the car for another minute and told me a few things.

"Don't consider yourself out of work yet. I'll talk to Alvin. I'll explain to him why you asked the questions you did. I'm sure he'll come around. After all, you were only concerned for our safety. But if Alvin won't listen to reason, I'll simply hire you on my own and pay the whole bill myself. Don't worry, things will work out. Anyway, give me a call this evening. And thanks for the ride."

She didn't wait for me to come around and open the car door for her. I watched her walk to the shop door where she turned and gave me a little wave before disappearing inside. After getting canned by Alvin, I'd been all ready to walk away from this case. Now I wasn't so sure. It was still early in the day, so I decided to go back to my office and hope that somebody would interrupt my nap by offering me some work.

That didn't happen, and so my nap lasted a lot longer than I'd planned. It was after six when I locked up to go home. But now I was awake, keyed up, and I didn't want to go back to my place just yet. Ambrosia was a poor conversationalist. I wasn't particularly hungry, either, but I knew that once I got home I wouldn't want to go out again, and the thought of eating my own cooking only made me hungry for someone else's. I decided to try Rocko's Kitchen again. After all, just because their coffee and donuts were indigestible, that didn't mean everything on their menu was inedible.

When I walked through Rocko's door, the same stale grease smell greeted me, and the same short, mean-looking, girl was behind the counter. I selected one of the red upholstered stools and sat down.

"You still here?" I asked.

"My shift ended hours ago, but I've been waiting here hoping you'd come by."

"I guess it's your lucky day."

"What can I get you, sport? The menu's on the wall behind me."

"You serve anything decent in this hole?"

"Try the meatloaf."

"It's good?"

"I don't know, I don't eat here. But we've got some meatloaf left over and I don't want to throw it out."

"Give me a hamburger. Just one patty, I don't want you to have to kill another horse. And fries. And coffee. Is the coffee fresh this time?"

"Boy, I'll say. It couldn't be fresher. It's tomorrow's coffee. We decided to make it early."

She stuck her frizzy head through a square hole in the back wall and shouted my order to whatever gorilla they had back there cooking. She came back and poured me a cup of coffee, carefully spilling it so I'd have something to dip my sleeve in later.

"Say, what's your name, buster?"

"You got it on the first guess. It's Buster."

"Really? Naw, it ain't. You look more like a Percy, or a Francis."

"To hell with you, sister. It's Axe."

"Axe? Pretty. Your mom must have wanted a little girl."

"I hope yours didn't."

"That's not nice." She put one pudgy claw over the nametag on her stylish smock. "Bet you can't guess my name."

"Is it Angel? Charity? Gardenia?"

"It's Tracy, you sap. How's the coffee?"

"I've had worse, but not since the war."

113

"They let you in the war? I bet you were a fighter pilot."

"No, just a regular dogface."

"At least you had the face for it."

I got an idea. I pulled out one of the prints of Roscoe's picture. "You ever see this guy?"

She squinted at the picture "No, never."

"You sure?"

"Could I forget an ugly mug like that? Who is it, your twin brother?"

"No, never mind. That burger and fries about ready?"

"You smell anything burning? No? Then your burger and fries aren't ready. Tell me about this guy in the picture. Why you looking for him?"

"It's my business."

"Fine, be that way."

Honest to God, she actually looked hurt.

"No," I said, "you took me wrong. This really is my business. I'm an investigator. It's what I do for a living, though, actually, it's more of a dying by slow starvation."

"You mean you're a private eye, like in the movies?"

I was horrified to see a look of actual admiration on her puffy face.

"No, not like in the movies. Like for real. Say, are you going to serve me that burger, or are you waiting for it to slide out here on its own grease?"

She turned to the hole in the wall, bellowed something incomprehensible, and returned with a shiny hamburger, and a pile of shinier fries, on a big platter.

"You ever carry a gun?" Tracy asked, pushing the ketchup bottle closer to me.

"Only when I eat here. You've got the biggest cockroaches in the county."

"Think so? It's a big county. Say, you ever need any help with your detective work, let me know. What'd this guy in the picture do? Something awful?"

"Pretty awful. He died. But what's even more awful, he might have come back to life."

"Now you're pulling my chain."

"No, I'll leave that to the zoo keeper."

"You going to pay for that?" She gestured with her favorite dirty rag at my now mostly empty plate.

I swallowed the last bite, stood up, and took out my wallet. I handed Tracy one of my business cards. She read it out loud.

"'Axel Hatchett, Private Investigator. No Nut Too Hard To Crack'"

"If you happen to see the guy in the picture I showed you, give me a call." I paid my tab, then slid a quarter across the counter. "Buy your boyfriend a new harmonica." I headed for the door.

"How'd you know he played the harmonica?" she asked in her scratchy voice. "He says it makes the jail time go faster."

"Nice to hear you're dating a guy with talent."

I walked out the door and returned to my car.

Either I'd been hungrier than I'd thought, or the hamburger at Rocko's had actually been good. I'd saved a couple of French fries, rolled up in a napkin, to give to Ambrosia when I saw her, but when I got home she was nowhere around.

I was wide awake and didn't know what to do with myself. I tried the television, but nothing interested me. I started to reread one of my favorite westerns, but I found myself reading the same lines over and over. It was too early to go to bed, and I was feeling too lazy to go out again.

At least I told myself it was laziness that kept me in. But I knew better. I was sticking around because I was hoping Rita would give me a call. I thought she would, but I didn't know how late it'd be. Of course, I could've called her myself, but that might have made me look like a chump.

Since I couldn't think of anything else to do to pass the time, I went to bed early. And, surprisingly, I fell asleep. But I hadn't been asleep more than half-an-hour when the phone started ringing. I stumbled out of bed and found my way to the phone in the living room.

11

"Hello?" I said, sounding as grumpy as I felt.

"Is that you, Axe? It's Rita." She sounded breathless. "You've got to help us. It's Roscoe. We've heard from him. He's going to kill Alvin. You were right."

I was still pretty groggy with sleep, so Rita's words caught me off guard.

"Your dead husband's going to kill his brother?"

"Yes, just as you suggested. He called Alvin on the phone. Alvin called me, and now I'm calling you. You have to stop Roscoe from killing Alvin."

"That's a pretty tall order for somebody who doesn't even work for you," I said, grumpily.

"Forget all that. Alvin's sorry, and he wants you back. And I never stopped wanting you. Will you help?"

She had a way with words, I'll give her that. But I wasn't flattered by her admission that I'd been right about Roscoe's murderous jealousy. Instead, I felt conned. What were Rita and Alvin up to? But I didn't want to let on that I was suspicious.

"What makes you think Roscoe is trying to kill Alvin?"

"He called him, I told you. Alvin wanted me to come over and stay with him. But I can't, not in that nosey neighborhood. Besides, what could I do?"

"How does Alvin know it was his brother on the phone? It could be some kind of joke, or prank. Maybe one of Alvin's poker buddies had a few too many beers tonight — "

"No. Alvin was sure it was Roscoe, even though his voice sounded different, raspier. Remember the scar on his neck in the pictures? He must have damaged his throat somehow, his voice box. But Alvin recognized him anyway. It was the way he talked, his speech pattern. And some of the favorite words he used. And he knew things about Alvin that only Roscoe could know, things about their childhood, and things about Alvin's time in the army that he hadn't shared with anyone but his brother. He told Alvin he was going to kill him, shoot him dead."

"Because he was jealous, like I guessed? He thought his supposed widow and his brother were romantically involved?"

"I'm not sure about that, really. Roscoe didn't say why he wanted to kill Alvin. But I thought you might be right, and Alvin agreed. Someone needs to go stay with him. I want it to be you."

"What about the cops? Did you call them?"

"Of course. I called them myself and told them what was going on. I might as well have asked them if they had Prince Albert in a can. They think Alvin and I are a couple of bored practical jokers. At least, that's how they treat us."

"Look, I don't have any great affection for Quartz Quarry's police force, but they aren't idiots, and they aren't lazy, and I doubt they're even especially corrupt. You must have got on their bad side somehow. If what you're telling me about your husband threatening your brother-in-law is true, the cops need to be involved. You need them. You want I should call them? I've actually got a couple of contacts on the force."

"Don't! Please. I lied to you, I'm sorry. I didn't call the police tonight. Partly because I didn't think they'd care, and because I'm afraid they might hurt Roscoe, kill him even. If they think he's just some crazy man, a murderer, they might shoot him to protect Alvin. "

"And you'd rather have Alvin killed."

"Of course not! I don't want anyone killed. "

"Then how are you going to stop it?"

"I can't. But I think you can. I'm hoping so. Please, time's running out. Alvin's all alone, and there's no telling when Roscoe might show up. He was a sniper in the war."

"I know that. Tell Alvin to keep his doors locked, his windows closed and latched, and his curtains closed. You told me he doesn't have a gun, but I know better. He has one at his shop, and he's probably got another one at home. Or he can pull up stakes and move in with you for a while, unless your neighbors are as nosey as his, in which case he can move into a hotel or motel for a time. There's lots of options. Alvin's not helpless. It's a game of cat and mouse, and you know how cats like to play with their food.

"And another thing, if Roscoe really wants to kill Alvin, then why would he warn him? Why not just shoot him and get it over with? I'll tell you why. He wants to watch Alvin sweat and worry, and grow scared. It doesn't matter that Roscoe was a sniper in the war. He's not going to shoot Alvin from ambush with some rifle he stole. If he shoots him at all, it will be from point-blank range. Trust me, Alvin just needs to lay low. A hotel room might be his best bet."

"I don't think he'll leave his house, at least not until daylight. Can't you just go over and stay with him for the rest of the night? I'll tell you where he lives, I'll even pick you up and take you there if you want. I wouldn't ask you if there was anyone else I could ask. Besides, I wouldn't want anyone but you handling the situation. I know you'll protect Alvin, and I know you won't hurt Roscoe. But promise me you'll be careful and not put yourself in danger."

I had to laugh at that. It probably wasn't a very pleasant sound. "Sure, Rita. I'll keep both Roscoe and Alvin safe, and I'll side-step any bullets that come my way."

"You're wonderful," she gushed. "Should I pick you up then? Say, half an hour?"

"Just give me directions, and tell Alvin I'm coming. I don't want him accidently shooting me, in case he does have a gun with him."

She gave me Alvin's address and I hung up, feeling like a chump. I was being suckered into some unholy game, but I wasn't sure what it was. Rita and Alvin were up to no good, that much was certain. And they were taking me along for the ride.

I drank some of that morning's coffee, cold, then scraped off the doormat that grows on my face every few hours, brushed my teeth, and got dressed. From under my bed I dragged out the double-barreled twelve-gauge shotgun I always keep there, broke it down into its three pieces, and took them and a box of shells out to the car with me. I had my thirty-eight stuck in my belt, and there was a Browning High Power in the glove compartment of the Hornet. I felt I was sufficiently armed to defend Alvin's castle against all invaders.

As I drove over to Alvin's neighborhood, I cursed myself again for not having a job with regular hours, like a fireman or a grave robber. It turned out to be harder to find Alvin's house than I'd expected. It was in an area that used to be small farms and orchards. Little by little, the land had been bought up and turned into rows and rows of houses, but some of the farmers and fruit growers had proved stubborn. They were waiting for their property taxes to go through the roof before they gave up and sold their properties. Alvin and Della's house was located in a small row of houses between a couple of the old orchards. There were trees everywhere, a lot more than I thought were necessary. To make up for the abundance of vegetation, there was a virtual lack of street lights.

The house was at the end of a long graveled drive with hedges on each side. There was a yellow porch light on, and some dim light coming through the closed front curtains, which must have been a reddish brown. With the addition of my headlights, I could guess that Alvin's residence was a smallish, two-storied, clapboard affair painted white, or cream, with a darker roof and shutters.

As I put my shotgun back together and loaded it, and took the pistol from the glove box, I saw one of the curtains twitch. I turned off the headlights and spent a few seconds looking around in the dark for dead men with guns before I got out and climbed the steps to the front door. I thumbed the doorbell and looked around some more, and came to the conclusion that this was a nice quiet spot to commit a murder. Alvin answered the door faster than I thought he would. He opened the door a crack and said, "What's the password?"

"Corned beef on an onion roll."

He laughed, way too much, and I realized he must have reached the friendly and hilarious stage of drunkenness. I was none too happy. I wasn't in the mood to trade silly stories with him for the rest of the night, and I might actually need him sober. He pulled the door all the way open and pushed the screen door my way. I went inside and he closed the door and locked it up tight with a deadbolt and one of those things on a chain.

"What's with all the locks?" I asked. "You live out in the sticks."

"I'm a locksmith, remember? You think I'm not going to have decent locks on my own doors?"

He said all this with a return to surliness that gave me hope he might not be as drunk as I'd feared. Not only that, I now saw he was holding a revolver, an old-fashioned, nickel-plated relic from the days of Billy the Kid.

"Rita told me you didn't own any guns. Counting the one you have in your paw, and the one you keep in your office, I'm guessing that makes two."

"Rita's right, I don't like the things. The one at the shop is left over from when my Dad ran the place. This one in my hand? A friend loaned it to me, just today. Really."

"You think I'm a sap?"

"Doesn't matter. Give me your hat and coat. You want a sandwich? A drink?"

"Nothing, thanks." I looked around. I couldn't

see much. Some furniture, drapes, a carpet, two small lamps in different rooms "You've got the place looking pretty dark, no silhouettes showing through the curtains. That's good. Tell me about your brother's phone call. Start with when it happened. Did you think it was Della?"

"No, she called a hell of a lot earlier. I didn't know who'd be calling so late. I thought it might be Rita, but it was him, Roscoe. I couldn't believe it." He put his hand to his forehead and massaged it, like he was trying to get rid of the memory. "Listen, let's go into the den — there's no windows in there."

I followed him from the living room, through an adjoining dining room, and through a doorway on the left into a room that was the size of a small bedroom. There was a miniature fireplace made of fieldstone, knotty pine paneling, and a couple of built-in bookcases with actual books in them. There was also a pair of pretty comfortable looking arm chairs with a small oak table between them. I couldn't help wishing I had a room like this at home. It looked peaceful and comfortable.

I leaned my shotgun against the wall near the fireplace, then I took the Browning nine-millimeter from where I'd tucked it in the small of my back and deposited it on the rough oak mantle. Alvin watched me with worried eyes.

"Why all the hardware? He's just one guy, and he's my brother."

"There's nothing like being over-prepared. Let

me take a gander at that hog leg you're toting." I reached out my hand and he dutifully surrendered the revolver.

I opened the side gate, pulled the hammer to half cock, and one by one spilled out five forty-five longs into my palm. The brass casings were tarnished, and the lead projectiles were a bit green and greasy, but they looked serviceable enough. The nickel plate on the gun was scratched and worn off in spots, and the walnut grips were cracked in a couple of places. Still, it had a well-oiled, well-cared-for feel.

I pulled the cylinder pin, dropped out the cylinder, and with the aid of the table lamp, and a corner of my white pocket-handkerchief, determined that the bore was clean, with no rust or pits. I reloaded it. Five bullets, six chambers.

I left the chamber directly under the hammer empty. With old revolvers of this type, if you dropped one, or if something struck the hammer accidently, the gun could go off. There were more than a few dead desperadoes who learned that lesson too late.

Among those cowboys who loaded only five rounds in their sidearms, there were a few gloomy members who kept a rolled-up five or ten dollar bill in that empty chamber to pay for their own funerals when the time came. I handed the gun back to Alvin. He took it back with shaking hands and dumped it on the lamp table between the chairs.

"Sit down." said Alvin. "Make yourself comfortable. And by the way, thanks for coming. I appreciate it, I really do. I'm sorry about, you know, the way I treated you earlier, in my shop. You made me mad, but I'm sorry. Honest."

"Forget it."

"Thanks. Say, you sure you don't want a drink?"

"I'm on duty. No"

"I'm going to have another."

He went over to one of the bookcases and swung open an array of fake books. Behind them were a couple of crystal decanters, a syphon bottle, and some short cut glass tumblers. There was also a silver ice bucket. So much for Alvin's reading. He selected a tumbler, grabbed one of the decanters, and poured a fulsome dollop of dark amber liquid with a shaking hand. He took the syphon bottle and squirted some fizzy liquid from it into his drink.

He turned to me. "No ice," he said with regret. "I ain't going to the kitchen for ice. And I ain't going to ask you to." He closed the secret door and sat down. "Cigarette?" He held out a white pack of Lucky Strikes. I shook my head.

"I'll have a cigar later," I told him, "if you don't mind."

"No, whenever you like." He lit his cigarette, then looked at his Lucky package. "Remember when Lucky Strike packages were green?"

I grunted.

"But then the war happened. Remember?"

"I remember. Then Lucky's ad campaign said 'Lucky Strike green has gone to war.' They sacrificed their green ink to dye dogface's uniforms."

"Yeah. That's why I smoke this brand. That was mighty patriotic of them."

"No doubt. I don't suppose it hurt their sales any, either."

"You're a glass-half-empty kind of guy."

"No. I'm a drink straight from the bottle, forget about the glass, kind of guy. So?"

"Nothing. I'm an optimist. I wish everybody was. What I'm saying is, I think all of this with Roscoe is going to work out. Pals come forward when you need them, you know?"

"According to you and Rita, your own brother is trying to kill you. What pals are you talking about?"

Alvin took a long guzzle from his half-full drink. "Milton, for one. He's the guy who loaned me the gun."

"Milton? This is Milton's shooting iron?"

Alvin shrugged. "I think the gun belonged to his aunt. She was a nurse."

"Sure, that explains things. How did Milton know you needed a gun?"

"Rita. After I called her and told her about Roscoe's threat, I guess she decided I needed a gun. I don't know how she thought of Milton. Anyhow, a little while ago he dropped by and gave me this pistol. I thought maybe he'd stay with me, but I think he's pretty scared of Roscoe. You know, because of his threatening to come by and kill me."

"Alvin, I need you to give me the details about this phone call. Did Roscoe actually say he was going to 'come by' and kill you here at your home?"

"I don't know. Let me think about it." He took another fulsome sip from his drink, and massaged the back of his neck. "It was late, and I was already asleep. I thought it might be Della again, but it was some guy. He had a kind of hissing voice, like a talking snake or something. Gave me the heebie jeebies. He was talking nonsense, saying he was going to kill me for sure, and that I knew why I deserved it. Some damned crank, I figured. I was getting ready to hang up, but something stopped me. I don't know, there was something about the way the guy talked that was familiar. It made the hair on my arms stand up, I swear. And I suddenly knew it was Roscoe, before he even told me."

"How?"

"It was something about the way he talked, kind of with a drawl. Our mom came from the south, and she kind of drawled. Roscoe picked it up, but I never did. Anyhow, instead of hanging up the phone, I kept listening. And pretty soon he proved to me he was Roscoe. "

"How?"

Alvin shrugged again. "He knew stuff about when we were kids. And he knew about my tattoo from the war."

"Lots of guys came back with tattoos, what's special about yours?"

"I got it when I was drunk. It's a monkey doing the hula. He's got a grass skirt on, a flower necklace, and a halo."

"Sounds like you weren't the only one drunk. Surely your brother isn't the only one who knows about your tattoo. What about your wife?"

He shook his head. "No, not even Della. Here, I'll show you." He proceeded to unbutton his shirt. He was as hairy as a bear in winter. "It's right over my heart. Can you see it?"

I took a good squint. I couldn't see a damn thing but fur. "What's the point? Why get a tattoo that nobody will ever see, even you?"

He laughed a little nervously "I wasn't always this hairy. That second year I was in the army they must have fed us some kind of miracle hair grower or something. By that time I already had the tattoo, but I never told anybody about it but Roscoe. I don't even know why I told him."

"OK, he knew about your tattoo. For the moment let's agree that it was really your brother on the phone. Why did he threaten to kill you? What reason did he give you? Any? And why would he warn you in advance?"

Buttoning up his shirt, Alvin shrugged once more. I found this repeated gesture annoying. "He never really said. He just kept saying I knew the reason. I don't know what he's talking about. He's not right in the head."

"Rita seems to believe her husband wants to kill you because you've been eying his widow. What do you think? Don't shrug."

"That's a possibility, I guess, though it doesn't make any sense. It ain't true, for one thing. And if it was true, what of it? Does a dead man have a right to get jealous over somebody's spending time with his widow? All that matters to me is that he wants to kill me. Shoot me. That's what he kept saying, he's going to shoot me. And it sounds like he wants to be looking me in the eye when he does it."

"It's not likely he'll follow you to work to shoot you — there's too much chance of interruption. But since he's telling you what he's going to do, why isn't he afraid of police interference? You know, none of it makes sense to me. If he wanted to talk with you before he put a bullet through you, he could simply pick the lock on your back door late one night and surprise you while you're snoring."

Alvin started to shrug and I pointed a warning finger at him. "Save your shoulder muscles. Does he want you to sweat in advance, do you think?"

"That could be. If that's what he wants, he's sure getting it." He drained his glass and I saw his hand shaking a little. I felt sorry for the poor slob.

"What do you want from me? I'm not a body guard. I'll stay here tonight, but that's it. Tomorrow you'll have to make other arrangements. If you want, I can give you the phone number of a guy who's an ex-cop and runs a small security agency. He's good at what he does, even if he sometimes believes he's some kind of Wyatt Earp."

"Sure, give me the guy's number. But he'll have to understand one thing, I don't want Roscoe hurt. Neither does Rita. That's why we hired you to track down my brother and give us a chance to bring him in alive. We still want you on the case, but no rough stuff when it comes to Roscoe. I mean, if it's necessary you can sap him, or bust his jaw, or cut him a little if you have to. But no rough stuff. If you got to grapple with him, or have a shootout, I want him taken alive. Understood?"

"Sure, pal, and after that I'll get a job catching lions for the zoos by picking them up by their scruffs and saying, 'bad kitty.'"

"Maybe you need to talk to Rita again. Mind if I have another drink?"

"It's your house. You can take a bath in it if you want. I'm not talking to Rita again. I know what a chump I am when it comes to dames like her. Let's face it, Rita could talk the right guy into doing just about anything. And I'm the right guy. This case stinks. It always has. You're keeping things back that I need to know. If you don't come clean, I'm going to walk."

Alvin rose and revisited the secret liquor cabinet, making another scotch and soda from his favorite recipe. He returned to his chair but didn't say a word for a good minute. A pretty impressive silence for a guy who obviously liked to talk. "OK, let's make a deal. I'll tell you a couple of things, but you got to keep them close to the vest."

"If it's anything illegal, forget it."

"Nothing illegal, not really. But there's a couple of things me and Rita don't want other people to know about. Especially Della."

12

I couldn't help it, I started laughing. Alvin gave me a dirty look, but I kept laughing anyway. He gulped down half his scotch. "So," I said, fairly crowing, "you wanted to pull a gun on me for what I said about you and Rita. And now you're about to tell me I was right. "

"OK, OK. Go ahead and have your laugh. Maybe I deserve it. But it still isn't what you think. Not exactly, anyway." He gulped down a bunch more of his scotch.

"You keep drinking that way and I'll have to take that gun away from you."

"Come on, you've got your own guns. Let me keep this one. It's not like I'm waving it around or anything."

"Make sure you don't. Now, go on with what you were telling me."

"We didn't mean to do it, believe me. But it was almost like it was fated, you know?"

"I don't believe in fate. I believe in opportunity

and luck. Your brother has an accident and his body's never found. You and Rita, the widow, are pretty broken up. Understandably, you end up spending a lot of time together. Nothing wrong with that. Then you get a little closer than you should, and that's not OK. You're married, and you don't even know for sure that Roscoe's dead."

"But we stopped it. It didn't last long. We did the right thing."

"So what's the problem? Roscoe? He reappears, hangs around, then calls you up and says he's going to kill you. Where's he been the last two years? Playing chess with himself? Why'd he come back, and how'd he find out about you and his wife?"

"I can't answer any of that. But I do know there's somebody who knew, who followed us, took pictures."

"Working for who? Della? Roscoe?"

"I don't think either."

"Freelance, huh? A blackmailer. Why didn't you tell me that? That's the kind of thing I could help you with."

"We don't need help now. We've already taken care of things."

"You mean you've paid the bastard off. If you think that's the end of it, you're wrong. I suppose he sold you the negatives of the pictures he took. That doesn't mean a thing. He could have a hundred prints you don't know about. He may leave you alone for a while, but as soon as he gets hungry, he'll be back. I hope I'm wrong, but I doubt it."

"We got things fixed, believe me. But we don't need anybody else knowing. Look, it cost me and Rita plenty to keep this peeper from showing his pictures around. Actually, it's been Rita's money the whole time because Della keeps track of every cent I spend. I don't know how she does it. But I found a way to pay Rita back, and then some. And as for the sewer rat who found us out and used it as a moneymaker, he knows what will happen if any of the pictures he took get into the wrong hands. In fact, he's going to be giving us back some of the money when he can scrape it together. What do you think of that?"

"You know the guy, the blackmailer? That makes things kind of interesting for everybody concerned, doesn't it?"

"Yeah. But everything's straightened out and taken care of. We don't want the cops sticking their noses in it or the whole story might get out. If the cops find out about the blackmail they'll investigate it, won't they? That's why we want to keep you."

"So you'd rather risk getting knocked off by your brother than have your wife find out about you and Rita. Do you believe that's how you ought to be thinking?"

"That's how it's going to be, as much for Rita's sake as mine."

The door to Alvin's den was open, and we could hear sounds from outside. Just then a scratching noise pricked up our ears, and a faint tapping. Probably nothing other than a gust of wind blowing through the branches of some tree or bush growing near a window, but Alvin jumped like he'd seen the devil coming down the chimney. He glanced at his gun but I shook my head.

"I'll take care of this," I said. I grabbed up the shotgun and made the rounds of the house, checking the door locks, peeking through window curtains. At one window I heard the tapping and scratching sound again. I pulled the curtain aside just enough to see the shape of a lilac bush in the near darkness. Just as I'd thought. Nothing to worry about. Not yet, anyhow.

I returned to the den. "It was nothing but a lilac bush playing at Halloween," I told Alvin, but he was back over at the liquor cabinet pouring a drink with one hand while he held his big revolver with the other. "Lay off that stuff! Who wants to babysit a rummy? Come on, put the gun down. "

He went back to his chair and dutifully deposited the gun on the lamp table, muzzle facing toward the fireplace. "I wish it was morning."

"You and me both. Dawn's not too far off. Maybe you ought to get some shuteye, as they say in the Westerns. You aren't going to be worth much at work if you don't. I'll stay on guard duty, don't worry."

"Do you really think I could sleep? I might wake up dead, with a bullet in me."

"Drink the rest of that hooch and hit the sack. It's the best thing for you."

"There's two windows in the bedroom. I'm not sleeping there."

"All right, then sleep on the couch in the living room. It's not too close to a window. I'll sit in a chair and watch over you, just like an angel. And don't worry, I won't fall asleep. I'll keep an open eye at all times. In fact, I'll let my eyes take shifts. First hour for the right eye, second hour for the left."

Alvin gave me a bleary, belligerent look. "Can't you ever be serious?"

"I'm always serious. Now go on, take a nap. You're getting on my nerves, drinking like a fish and waving that gun around."

His face flushed redder than it'd already been. "Don't tell me what to do in my own house," he warned.

I shook my head. "I sure don't see how Rita ever had you pegged as some kind of fun-loving guy. Hell, I've known hard-shell Baptist temperance spinsters with better senses of humor than yours. I've got half a mind to walk out on you right now."

He stood up unsteadily and reached for his revolver. I beat him to it, but he managed to knock it out of my hand. It hit the floor with a metallic thump. I was a second away from applying a fist to Alvin's jaw when I saw all the fight drain out of him.

"Sorry," he said. "You're right, I need to get some rest. Wake me if anything happens." He wandered into the darkened living room and collapsed on the couch, his face turned to the backrest. I followed and settled myself in a big wing chair that smelled of dust. Within a couple of minutes Alvin was snoring. Good, I thought, at least I'll have something to keep me awake.

I spent the rest of the night sitting in my chair with a throw pillow behind my neck, listening for the sounds of breaking glass, or splintering wood or locks being picked, and watching the sky grow lighter behind the closed drapes in the living room.

Alvin slept the whole time; things were kind of peaceful. A couple of times I felt myself beginning to nod off, but visions of Roscoe, sniper rifle clamped in lunatic paws, creeping through stands of fruit trees, a look of maniacal glee on his face, pulled me awake each time.

On another occasion, as I half dozed, I saw in my mind's eye the figure of Roscoe creeping into the living room, smiling at the rumpled figure of the detective, slumped in his chair, slack jaw emitting faint snores, a shiny line of spittle staining the chair upholstery. As he raised the rifle, a veritable elephant gun, and aimed it at the spot where my brain ought to be, I jerked myself awake. I was pretty happy when the sky lightened enough so I could call it morning.

I stumbled my way to the kitchen and looked

for coffee makings. I found them.

By the time the coffee had finished percolating, I heard Alvin stirring around in the living room. In a couple of minutes, he joined me in the kitchen.

"Looks like we both made it through the night," I said, cheerfully enough.

"I guess that's so. Is that coffee I smell?"

"Sure is. Care for a cup? Cream? Sugar?"

"Sugar, lots of it."

I dug around in the cupboards and found two cups. There was a canister of sugar on the counter. We drank our coffee in silence, both standing up. When we'd finished our second cups, Alvin said, in a croaky voice, "I got to get ready for work. You'll stay here till I'm ready?"

"Sure, I've got no place else to go. Take your time."

To my surprise, he reached into a cabinet under the sink and extracted a dark brown bottle with a festive label. Some kind of rum I figured.

"Christmas present," he muttered. "Want some?" I shook my head and he uncorked the bottle and poured a measure into his empty coffee cup. He drank it down in one swallow, but he didn't look like he enjoyed it.

"You might want to watch that hair-of-the-dog stuff," I suggested. "I wouldn't want you choking on a fur ball."

He nodded. "Want some breakfast?"

"You feel like eating?"

"I got to get something in my stomach besides this." He nodded at the rum bottle.

"Sure, breakfast sounds fine. Who's buying?"

"Buying? I'll cook it myself." And damned if he didn't grab a big barbecue apron from a broom closet and tie it on.

His cooking was scarier than anything that had happened the night before. He knew his way around a kitchen just well enough to set fire to every combustible edible he touched. I made more coffee and played fireman while Alvin put together a meal of charred toast, burnt bacon, and overcooked fried eggs with black edges. We ate in silence while the smoke cleared, sitting in a little breakfast nook.

Alvin looked at his watch, a nice gold one with an alligator band, and said, "I got to get ready for work. I'll just take a quick shower and dress. Wait for me, I won't be long. Use the telephone if you want. Call Rita, tell her what's going on. Say, how come she hasn't called me? Don't she care if the two of us got shot last night?"

"Maybe she's afraid to find out."

"Maybe. Give her a ring, I know she'll want to hear from you."

He disappeared through one of the kitchen's two doorways and I heard the water start running. I found the phone in the living room and dialed Rita's number. It rang five or six times before she answered.

"Hello?" she said. Her voice was sleepy, sultry.

"Thought I'd let you know Alvin is still alive and kicking."

"And you too. That's great. What happened last night?" Her voice had perked up considerably.

"Nothing happened, and that's OK by me. Alvin's getting ready for work. I'm going to follow him to his shop and make sure nobody's waiting there for him."

"Good idea. And then you can come over to see me. I'm not going into work until late. Come over, I'll give you breakfast."

"I already ate, thanks. Alvin whipped something together."

"I'm sorry."

"Yeah. If you look out the window you might still be able to see the smoke. Anyway, after I escort Alvin to work I'm going home to get an hour or two of sleep."

"Come over here before you go home. I feel, I don't know... edgy."

"You're fine."

"Please."

"You won't like me the way I am. I slumped in a chair all night. My clothes are wrinkled. My face is covered with bristles, and I no doubt smell like a trip to the zoo."

"Sounds sweet. I'm still in my nightgown and robe, if that makes you feel any better."

"I'm sure you look a whole lot better in your nightie than I do in my rumpled clothes."

"I'm not wearing makeup and I haven't done

anything with my hair. Hurry over. I want to make sure we have enough time to talk before I go to work."

"OK, you asked for it. I'll see Alvin to his door and head straight to your place. Don't sic the dog on me."

"There's no dog. I'm all alone. Let me give you directions."

I was writing down the directions and the address when Alvin reappeared. He was dressed for work in gray pants, a pink and charcoal dress shirt, and polished black shoes. His hair was slicked down and still wet, and his face looked like something you'd put in the window at Halloween. I hung up the phone and said, "Stay away from the bug juice today. It's not doing you any good."

He agreed. The two of us left the house. I checked out Alvin's Studebaker to make sure there was no Roscoe lurking in the backseat. Then we headed out in our separate cars, both aiming for Ravencamp's Keys and Locks. It wasn't a long drive, and when we got there I went inside with him to check for ambushers. I didn't find any.

"Stay close to the shop today," I advised him. "I'll get you the name and number of that security guy I know and call you later. Right now I'm headed out to Rita's."

"Good idea," he said, and I left.

13

Rita's directions led me to a pretty nice neighborhood, more snooty than Alvin's, though not as private. I parked halfway around the circular drive, in front of a pink brick, one-story house with some big windows. It was a pretty good-sized place, with some flower gardens and trees growing around it. To one side was a two car garage with the same maroon Ford I'd seen at Karl's parked in front of it.

When I rang the doorbell, I couldn't hear the chimes, and it was half-a-minute before the front door opened and Rita beckoned me in. The living room was big enough to hold dog races in. There was a lot of blond furniture and a cream carpet that someone had forgotten to mow.

"You look like a hobo," Rita laughed, inviting me to sit next to her on a nice little settee with a glass-topped coffee table in front of it. On the table was a silver coffee pot with matching cream pitcher and sugar bowl. A wisp of steam was snaking from the coffee pot's spout, so I figured Rita had just made it.

"I warned you about how I'd look," I said, pouring coffee for both of us into porcelain cups so thin I half expected them to shatter from the weight of the coffee.

"And I warned you about the way I'd look," she said, smiling.

She was wearing some sort of quilted satin wrapper, green, and it went very nicely with her green eyes and the red hair she had tied up in a loose ponytail. Without makeup she showed off a lot of nice freckles. She looked like a high school cheerleader, only a lot more dangerous. I wasted a moment wondering what it'd be like waking up next to a face like hers each morning. That wasn't ever going to happen.

"You couldn't look bad if you wanted to, could you?" I asked her.

"I'll take that as a compliment."

"Do."

"You drink your coffee black. I'm a cream and sugar girl myself."

"You sure are. I don't mind my coffee with cream and sugar. Or just cream. Or only sugar. I'm easy to please."

"That's a good trait. I wish Roscoe had been more like that."

"You're speaking about him in the past tense. Why?"

"Oh, I know he's alive. I just don't expect him

to be the same man he used to be. He's clearly been through a lot."

"I didn't see hide nor hair of him last night."

"I feel sorry for him, I do, even though he might have turned into a killer."

"Be careful. He's not the same guy you married. We need to find him, but I don't like the idea of using Alvin as bait. There's got to be a safer way to catch Roscoe. I know you don't like me talking about him like he's a wild animal, but that's the way we should be talking about him right now. Can you understand that?"

"I suppose I don't have a choice, but it's hard. Where is he living, I wonder, if you can call it living? In some other abandoned building downtown, do you suppose?"

I shook my head. "Naw, I figure he's living a lot closer to Alvin now that he's decided to kill him. He could be holed up in some old barn or something. There're plenty of nice hidey-holes in Alvin's neighborhood. I'm going to spend part of my day seeing if I can find Roscoe's new lair. I don't figure many of the property owners will be cooperative, so I'm not going to tell them."

"Be careful. Some old farmer might shoot you full of rock salt and bacon rind, or worse."

"I'll be careful, don't you worry."

"And dogs. Some of those country folk keep some pretty mean dogs."

"I'll wear a suit of armor, don't worry."

"Just like a knight."

"Stop it. Anything else?"

"Yes. Roscoe's not going to want to be interfered with. Not now."

"I agree. That brings us to the matter of Alvin's safety. I've already told him that I'm not bodyguard material. Last night was all right. I know things happened in a hurry. But now you've got all day to find a real protector. I've told Alvin about an ex-cop I know who runs a security business. I'll call him and then let you and Alvin know if he's available. And I'll give you his number so you can talk to him yourself. But if you want to go it alone just say so."

"By all means, give us any help you can. Let me get a pen and paper."

She rose from the settee and walked the length of the big living room, disappearing for a moment into another room then returning with a pad of paper and a pen.

I watched every step she took. There was something wickedly liquid about the way she moved, especially her walk. When she was nervous and jittery, as she'd been in my office when we'd first met, she lost a lot of her attraction. She certainly wasn't nervous today.

I wrote down the guy's name, though I didn't know his number off hand.

She didn't sit back down, and I took that as my cue to get going. She walked me to the front door. "Be careful today," she told me.

"I'll do my best."

"Of course you will. I have complete confidence in you."

I was on my own, crunching across the graveled drive to my car. I was glad somebody had confidence in me, because I sure didn't. I got behind the wheel of my noble Hornet and, as I sometimes do in moments of insecurity, began talking to it. "Sting, old fellow, it's up to you and me now. Don't let me down. No oil leaks. Understand?"

Though I was exhausted, I drove back out to Alvin's neighborhood and began looking for a likely place for a homeless killer to hole up. The area was pretty well filled up with newer houses like Alvin's, but a mile or so down the road from his place was an old farm that hadn't been touched. There were some "Posted, No Trespassing" signs nailed to the wooden posts of the old wire fence here and there, and there was a big flashy "For Sale" sign at the spot where the private drive met the public road, but the sign looked old.

I wondered why some real estate investor hadn't snatched up the property, but maybe the owner was holding out for the right price. From the road I could see a big, weathered barn, part of its roof gone. A ramshackle house sprawled alongside of it. And there were a couple of low outbuildings that might once have housed chickens or pigs.

The gate across the drive was locked. I'd have to walk in, but that was OK; I didn't exactly want to advertise my presence. I found a shady spot to park my car, then I walked up the road a little farther. I soon came to a spot where a dense hedgerow separated an old pasture from what once had been corn fields, or wheat fields, or whatever. The hedgerow ran in the direction of the house. It looked like a good arrangement for me to approach the farm house without drawing attention.

I stepped to the far side of the hedge, using it as cover while I approached the house. When I got about sixty feet away, I stopped and watched the old place for a good fifteen minutes, looking for any kind of movement and listening for any kind of sound that might indicate that the place was not entirely abandoned. Nothing.

I had no choice now but to walk in the open. So, as nonchalantly as I could manage, I sauntered over and stepped onto the porch. The front door and windows were boarded up on both sides of the house. I circled the house. The windows on both sides, and the back door, were also boarded up. There was a coal cellar, but the door was tightly battened down. I swallowed my disappointment and went on to examine the sheds.

One shed turned out to be an old hog pen that was boarded shut, but when I came to the second shed — a chicken coop — I found that it's door had been pried open, though perhaps not recently. Eureka, I thought. I pulled my little thirty-eight from its waistband holster and slipped into the coop.

Why am I always forgetting my flashlight? Then I remembered that I'd left it in Roscoe's downtown lair. I struck a match. The floor was so littered with broken farmyard tools, equipment, and other flotsam that I couldn't see how any self-respecting hen could have lived here, but the coop still smelled strongly of unbathed fowls. Not a pleasant odor. I couldn't imagine Roscoe, with his big nose, squashed or not, staying in this place if he had any choice. I decided to examine the barn next.

The grass between the chicken coop and the barn was long and dry. I made quite a bit of noise thrashing through it, but it couldn't be helped. If there was anybody at home in the barn, I was giving him more than a fair warning. Its gray board siding was rotted and kicked-in in places, which was how I gained entrance to the old building.

I lit more matches. There were some old hay bales, a claw-foot bathtub, and the rusty remains of a Model A flatbed truck. There was also an old wringer washing machine, a cream separator, and some old milk cans. That was pretty much the whole inventory.

I found the ladder that led up to the loft, and I put my foot on the bottom rung, but it broke easily under the pressure. The next rung behaved the same way. Nobody could be in that loft. I climbed back out into the open air, dusted myself off as best I could, and decided I'd done my best. This was not Roscoe's hideout. I went ahead and walked down the dirt drive back to the road. I no longer cared if anybody saw me.

I spent the next couple of hours driving along the main road and exploring a series of side roads. I didn't find any more deserted farms, but there were plenty of derelict outbuildings to investigate. I kept coming up empty. At one homestead I got chased off by a couple of slavering hounds. At another, a beefy housewife stood on her porch with her arms crossed and attempted to incinerate me with her dour glare.

By this time I was almost asleep on my feet, but I made one more stop before going home. I checked out Alvin's place. All was quiet. I examined the windows and doors, including the garage doors, and looked for any signs of attempted entry. There was nothing. I decided it was time to head home, get a couple of hours of sleep, and get back in the game. I was ready to get to the end of this case. Nothing much had gone my way so far, and things were getting dangerous. If it wasn't for Rita, I would have given up on this case even before Alvin fired me. I wished I could get a lasso on Roscoe, but I'd have to find him first.

On my way home I stopped for gas, and while the bugs were being washed off my windshield I used the pay phone to call Alvin before I forgot. He wasn't at his shop. I wasted another coin calling him at home. No answer. I called Rita at work.

"Rita's Art and Such," a guy answered. It was that Milton character, the swish.

"Is your boss there?"

"Can you wait a moment while I get her? Is this important?"

"Yes to both questions. Tell her it's Axe."

"Lovely. I'll tell her. Have patience. It's a virtue, if you hadn't heard."

Fruit, I thought, but I didn't say it. I listened to silence for a good solid minute before a breathless voice came on the line that was a whole lot more musical than Milton's.

"Yes?"

"I just wanted to tell you I didn't find a thing. No burrows for Roscoe. Just a bunch of empty farm buildings. I wonder if Roscoe's got hold of a car somehow."

"Oh, lord, I hope not."

"Me too. I wanted to tell Alvin, but he's not at work, and he's not at home."

"He's probably out on a job. I hope he's OK. You don't think he's…?"

"No, I don't. I figure he's at lunch or something. I'm in a phone booth at the gas station. I just looked up the number for my buddy who does security. Write it down and pass it on to Alvin when you reach him. I'm going home to get some sleep. If anything important comes up, call me. Don't worry about waking me."

"I'll call you if there's a reason. Go on and get some sleep."

I paid for my gas and realized that I was hungry. I'd had nothing to eat since Alvin's dubious home-torched breakfast. Tired as I was, I didn't relish the idea of whomping up something for lunch at my place. The cupboard was mostly bare, and I don't have a high opinion of my cooking skills, so I decided to stop off someplace and grab a bite.

How I ended up at Rocko's Kitchen I'm not quite sure. It wasn't the food, or the service, or the prices, or that special Rocko's ambience. It wasn't even anywhere near where I worked or lived. A horrible thought passed through my mind that I might have mistakenly developed something re-sembling feelings of affection for the cantankerous Tracy. But I assured myself that couldn't possibly be. Fate could never be so cruel.

"What'll it be today, Mr. Private Eye?" the fa-miliar dulcet screech greeted me as I walked through the door of Rocko's dog-food shop.

"Do you live here, or what?" I slid onto what I now thought of as "my" stool.

She pointed a reptilian thumb at the ceiling. "I sleep up there. I got a room. I even got a window. I'm always in this building. I'll probably die here."

"Grow your hair out and change your name to Rapunzel and I might be able to help you with that."

"You hungry, or did you just stop by to bat your eyelashes at me?"

"Speaking of bats, what's on the menu?"

"The usual. We're so perfect we don't ever change. How about another hamburger?" She leaned over the counter and leered at me.

"I just want a couple of egg sandwiches, if you can manage."

"Coming right up. You want coffee?"

"Is the current batch still in liquid form, or will I have to eat it with a fork?"

"Hey, just because it's you, I'll make a fresh pot."

She leaned into the hole in the wall behind her and shouted my order to the invisible cook, then she went about making coffee. "You look terrible," she told me. "I mean, worse than usual. The tax man finally catch up with you?"

"No. Father Time. I'll be all right as soon as I get a couple of hours of sleep under my belt."

"You need a shave. But, you know, maybe you should let your beard grow. You'd look better. Folks wouldn't be able to see as much of your face."

"Sure, maybe you're right."

"Hey, you're no fun today. What's wrong? What happened to all the charm? You haven't even insulted me. There's not somebody else, is there?" There was a look of concern in her squinty, mud-brown eyes. Or maybe it was just a look of suspicion.

"I'm just worn out, that's all. I need a nice quiet job like yours."

"It's not so quiet. Not lately, anyhow We had some real excitement the other night. Somebody could have been killed."

"With the kind of hash you sling, I should think death is a real possibility for all of your customers."

"Yeah? If you think the food's so bad, how come you keep coming back? Is it me?"

"I'm trying to build up my resistance to poisons. But never mind that. What happened here the other night?"

"A robbery, almost. Guy comes in here, sits down right where you're sitting, and orders a glass of water. I told him to go find a fire hydrant. I told him we weren't some kind of canteen, but more of a cantina. He didn't get the joke. He said he'd give me a nickel if I gave him the water, so I said, sure. Five cents is five cents."

Something like the growl of a wounded coyote came from the kitchen, and Tracy went to the hole in the wall and brought back my egg sandwiches. Then she poured me a cup of honest to God fresh coffee. "So, I turn to get this guy his glass of water, and when I turn back around, he's got a gun pointed at me. So I screamed. Like this." She let out a squawk that must have raised the dead in cemeteries throughout the county.

"What kind of gun? Some kid's cap pistol?"

"No, it was the real thing. A big, ugly revolver. I looked right at it. I could see the bullets in the chambers. It almost scared me. He ordered me to put all the cash we had in the place into this paper bag he brought. I said no. And then he pulled the trigger. Boy was he mad when the gun didn't go off. Me, I wasn't so mad."

"This guy actually tried to shoot you?"

"I'll say, and Cookie too. When I screamed, Cookie stuck his head out to see what was going on, and the guy, the robber, pointed his gun at Cookie and pulled the trigger again. Maybe five, six, times. Nothing. Nada, as they say in France." Tracy started wiping down the counter with, I swear, the same damned plague-ridden rag she'd been using the first time I saw her.

"Keep that thing away from me," I said, biting into my second sandwich.

She shrugged, and put the rag away. She leaned on the counter again, her breasts looking like albino beefsteak tomatoes stuffed in a bra. "The guy, the robber, he cursed us and ran out the door. "

"You were lucky. What'd the guy look like?"

"Short, ugly. Kind of like you, only better dressed."

"You called the cops?"

"No. For what? No crime was committed. Unless pointing a gun at someone and pulling the trigger is illegal."

"I think it just might be. Listen, you need to get your own gun."

She gave me a big wink and a smirk, then reached under the counter and produced a single-shot shotgun, maybe a twenty gauge, that looked like it might have been new the day General Grant was born. The barrel was rusty and the cracked stock had been repaired with a long winding of copper wire.

"Does that thing still shoot?" I asked.

"You bet it does. I took it out the other day and ran half a box of shells through it."

"Good. Listen, I've got to get to bed." I reached for my wallet, and Tracy stuck her open palm in my face. "On the house, Dick Tracy."

"I can't let you do that."

"Fine, go to hell."

I frowned at her, left my wallet where it was, and worked a quarter out of my pants pocket. I slid it across the counter. "Buy your boyfriend another harmonica."

She slid the quarter right back to me. "How many harmonicas does he need? He's only in for twenty years. So long, trooper."

14

My car was still waiting for me at the curb. I drove it home. The contents of my mailbox was disappointing. No checks, several bills. I went inside my log cabin, pulled off my shoes, and collapsed on my bed.

The fact that I had intermittently snoozed in the same clothes the night before did not inspire me to undress and don pajamas. I briefly considered setting my alarm clock for two hours, but I decided that particular instrument of torture needed a rest. If anyone needed me before I was finished with my nap they could nag me by telephone. I closed my eyes and counted exactly one sheep, though a pretty big one, before falling asleep.

When the phone rang and woke me up my first thought was that I'd overslept. But one glance at the daylight leaking through the closed blinds of my bedroom window showed me I hadn't pulled a Rip Van Winkle. I answered the phone. It was Rita.

"What are you doing?" she asked.

"Well, I was taking a well-deserved nap, but I guess that's over."

"Oh, don't be cross. I was wondering if you wanted to do anything with me."

"Such as?"

"Well, it's almost dinner time. I know a sweet little restaurant where we can spend your money."

"You sound awfully chipper. Why aren't you wringing your hands over the plight of your brother-in-law?"

"I've done that, and I can't do it anymore. I've talked to Alvin, over the phone, but that just makes things worse. I'm afraid he's angry with me."

"Why would that be?"

"Oh, I think because the man who wants to kill him is also my husband."

"That's ridiculous. He might as well be mad at himself because he's Roscoe's brother. You want me to try and talk some sense into him?"

"No, the last thing he wants right now is to be sensible. But I'm at loose ends. Couldn't you spare me some of your time?"

"I guess we both need to eat, huh? But don't trap me into going to some fancy restaurant. They'll throw me out for chewing my food with my mouth open."

"Italo's isn't like that. Just a quiet little place where the food is good. I could meet you there. Or you could pick me up. What do you say? Do you like Italian?"

"I like Gina Lollobrigida."

"What guy doesn't?"

"I'll pick you up. But it's going to be a good hour. If you thought I looked like a hobo this morning, you ought to see me now. I'll need time to pour some water over myself, and scrape the crab grass off my face. Is an hour OK?"

"Yes. I'll see you in an hour." She rang off.

Sure, I'm a chump. I've told you that before. I can't say "No" to some dames. I took way too long showering, shaving, brushing off my jacket, knotting my tie. And after all that, I still looked like me. Some things you just can't fix. Still, despite all my pointless preparations, I still managed to pull into Rita's curved drive in about sixty minutes.

Rita didn't make me wait. I was just ringing the doorbell when she opened the door and stepped out. She was wearing a black-and-white dress, her hair down and unfettered. Simple. She looked great. I was only sorry I didn't.

"Your hair's still wet," she said, smiling. "What's the point of driving a convertible if you can't use it to dry your hair?"

"I've got the top up just for you."

"How sweet."

I helped her into the passenger's seat, then went around and installed myself behind the wheel. "Where to, madam?"

She laughed, and gave me directions to the restaurant.

Italo's was what I expected it to be. A crumbling hole-in-the wall with inconvenient parking. Inside, it had a low ceiling, red-and-white checked table cloths, and dim light provided mostly by candles stuck in empty chianti bottles on each of the tiny tables. A fat guy with an accent as Italian as a big block of mozzarella showed us to a table for two. Hell, they all looked like tables for two.

I ordered spaghetti. I always order spaghetti in Italian restaurants even though I sometimes end up with ketchup and hamburger on a pile of cold noodles. I was lucky this time. They served me the real thing. And Rita's food looked good too. She ordered some kind of veal dish, with capers and cheese.

She offered to split a bottle of wine with me, but I demurred, sticking with my usual coffee, while she ordered wine by the glass. Before our food arrived, I sipped my strong coffee while Rita toyed with her wine.

"So what are we here to talk about?" I asked.

"Let's talk about you, Axe. I want to know all about you."

"Naw, I'm pretty tired of that subject. Let's talk about you, or cars, or baseball."

"You aren't getting off that easy. Come on, tell me your story."

I looked around the dark little restaurant. "Nice place. You come here often, with other detectives?"

"Never. I haven't been here for a while. I used

to have lunch here fairly often, with Ethel, my mother-in-law. I'm lucky, Ethel was easy to get along with. In fact, we were pretty good friends."

"I heard both Roscoe's folks are dead. Sounded kind of tragic, actually."

"Yes. Gus, my father-in-law, was killed in a hunting accident. Some deer hunter, probably full of beer, shot him by mistake. But the coward never came forward to admit it."

"It happens. That's why I don't go hunting. One reason, anyhow."

"Make sure you never take it up."

"And the mom, Ethel, she killed herself?"

"No! Where did you hear such a lie?" She looked mad when she said this. Her face was flushed, and her pretty nostrils flared.

"Sorry, didn't mean to get you all riled. I don't know where I heard that. I talk to a lot of people. Maybe it was Alvin who told me about his mom."

"I can't imagine he'd say such a thing. He can't possibly believe that. The truth is, Ethel had a bad back. She hurt it horseback riding. I was with her that day. Her horse got spooked by something and threw her. After that she was in pain most of the time. Her doctor prescribed pills for pain, and so she could sleep. I'm afraid she took more of them than she should have, the pain was so bad.

"One night she took way too many and she never woke up. I was the one who found her." There was a quaver in her voice and her eyes were shiny with tears.

I felt like a heel. "I'm sorry, I didn't mean to bring up a bad subject."

She forced a smile. "Ethel's not a bad subject, just a sad one. Let's talk about something else. Let's get back to talking about you."

"If you insist," I said, squirming in my chair a little, looking for a way out. I got lucky, because just then this swarthy-looking guy, wearing a shiny dinner jacket, striped pants, a cummerbund, and a red bow tie, stopped at our table and shook his fiddle at us. He'd been making the rounds of the restaurant, trying to pick up a few bucks playing sappy songs for moonstruck couples. Rita tried to wave the guy away, but I liked the idea of his sawing out a song for us, preferably a long one.

"What can I play for you so lovely a couple?" he asked, in a voice like a cat's purr.

"Let me think about it," I said. "Say, do you know any good cowboy songs? Can you play us 'Little Joe The Wrangler's Sister Nell'?"

"Ah, no."

"How about 'The Wreck Of The Old '97', or 'Jim I Wore A Tie Today'?"

"Sorry, I don't know this ones. A nice Italian song maybe. Yes?"

"An Italian cowboy song? Sure, let 'er rip."

Rita started laughing, and waved the guy away. He looked pretty disappointed.

"You just took the bread sticks right out of his kids' mouths," I complained.

"I did not. Come on, tell me your life's story."

162

"Oh, all right. I was raised on a farm, for real. In Kansas. It got kind of boring after a while. During my senior year of high school I fell for one of my classmates, a divine number named Opal Cramsy. She had aspirations, and I don't think they much included me. Anyhow, after graduation she went off to college at Alligator U in Florida."

"There's no such place."

"Maybe not, but it was one of those colleges in Florida. And guess what? I decided I wanted to go there too. Opal had some kind of scholarship. I had nothing. I got a job in a gas station and made enough to pay for my tuition and books and a little left over for an occasional bite to eat.

"I hadn't been in college long — I hadn't even decided on a major — when the war came along and got in the way of things. The Army sent me my draft notice, and Opal and I shared a tearful farewell. Actually only one of us shed tears, and it wasn't her. So that was the end of my higher education.

"I kept working at the gas station until I shipped out, and something interesting happened while I was there. One night a guy came in with a sawed-off shotgun. He took all our cash and a pair of tires. The cops weren't able to do much, so I tackled the case myself. I was able to track the guy down, help him into a nice jail, and recover some of the cash and both tires, though one of them was flat.

"My boss was pretty happy, and even gave me

a ten buck reward. That was my first detective work, though I didn't think about it again until after the war."

"What did you do when you got out of the Army?"

"I did what a lot of guys did, I went home. But Kansas didn't have much to offer me any longer. I remembered why I got tired of the place, bought a car, and started driving. I only had a few bucks in my pocket, but they lasted me all the way to California. San Francisco became my new home.

"I got a job selling used cars. I didn't much care for the work, but I did like living near the ocean. One day an old Army buddy showed up at the car lot where I was working. He was looking for a couple of used cars that ran well and had plenty under the hood, but were as inconspicuous as possible. He said the best colors would be brown or gray, but white or black would work, too. He'd just have to let them get good and dusty. That peaked my curiosity, believe me."

"Did your friend run a detective agency or something?"

"Bingo. I found a car he liked, an invisible old Dodge, tan, with no distinguishing dents or dings, and a well-cared-for engine. I told him about the gas station robbery I'd helped solve, and asked him if he could train me. He told me he'd keep me in mind if one of his other operatives quit or got killed."

"Killed? Did that ever happen?"

"Sure. But plenty of people want to kill used car salesmen, too, so I didn't figure turning gumshoe would be any more dangerous for me."

Our waitress came by and refilled my coffee cup and sold Rita a cup as well.

"I gather your friend in San Francisco eventually found a spot for you," said Rita, pushing me to keep talking.

"He did. It took a couple of months, but it was worth waiting for."

"Did you replace someone who'd been killed?"

"Naw, nobody got killed. Some guy just disappeared one day. It took me a while to learn the ins and outs of the job, but I think I got pretty good at it. I kept that job for years."

"That was in San Francisco, way out in California. How'd you end up in our little town?"

"I'd just as soon not talk about it. I've told you enough about me. Let's skip the rest of the story, OK?"

She gave me her best smile. At least I hope it was her best, because if she had a better one, guys like me wouldn't have a chance. "Now I'm all curious. Tell me the rest — how'd you end up leaving San Francisco for Quartz Quarry?"

"OK, here's the part I'm not too happy about. Like I said, I worked for the Piercing Eye Detective Agency for years. I liked the work well enough, and the pay wasn't bad. But somewhere along the way I stepped on some toes. Big toes. One day I was working on a case, feeling just fine, and the next day I was in jail for a crime I never even thought of committing. I was in for a year. Thank God for the prison library! You never know what books are going to end up in such a place. You have to wonder if anyone even looks at them before they go on the shelf."

"Prison. That must have been awful. No wonder you're always in such a sour mood."

"Who, me? I always thought I was pretty easy to get along with."

"In jail, maybe. Did somebody frame you? What happened?"

"Like I said, I stepped on some toes. My bloodhound's nose must have been sniffing around somebody who didn't want to be sniffed. I'm probably lucky they didn't just kill me. Instead, I got a year of hard time as a warning. And when I got out — on the very day I got out, and had just rented a hotel room to stay in — a guy shows up with an envelope for me. An ugly guy. He looked like a car had run over his face when he was a baby. He handed me the envelope and said, 'The boss says "scram".' That was it."

Rita leaned across the table and I could see the candlelight flickering in her green eyes. "What was in that envelope?"

"Money. A big stack of bills, enough to buy a pretty swell car, fill it with gas, and drive it far, far, away from San Francisco and California. The money was intended to buy me off. It worked."

"But did you ever figure out what it was you

supposedly knew? Did you ever learn what you were punished for, or paid off for?"

"No, and I'll be very happy if I die not knowing. That is, if I die of natural causes."

"Well, I think you had a close call. I'm surprised you stayed in the detective business."

"You know, I was thinking of getting out of it, trying something new, like worm farming, or skywriting, but luck wasn't on my side. I was just passing through Quartz Quarry, looking for a short-term job that could make me enough dough to keep on traveling. It was summer, and I got a job driving a popsicle truck. All day long I crawled through the streets, 'Beautiful Dreamer' playing endlessly in my ears, a bunch of screeching kids chasing me with their fists full of sticky nickels. Ever read Dante?"

"No. Did you read him in college, or prison?"

"Damned if I remember. But while the job lasted, I stayed in a little motor hotel out on the highway. One night the guy staying in the cottage next to mine was murdered. The guy who owned the motel was pretty upset about it. He figured it was bad for business, and he hoped the killer would get caught real soon and put away so his renters wouldn't be afraid of the place. I told him I had a bit of experience in the detective game, and he said he'd pay me to solve the murder if I could do it in a month. That is, if the cops hadn't solved the case by then.

"In two weeks I had the killer caught. I had

some luck; the killer was an idiot and left all kinds of clues behind him. The motel owner gave me two-hundred bucks, cash, and told me I could stay in one of his cottages rent free all winter if I wanted to. So I stayed in Quartz Quarry and eventually hung out my shingle as a private eye.

"And I'm so glad you did."

"Listen, isn't it about time we got out of this place? We've been here longer than the fiddler."

"I guess you're right. We should go. But I'm not looking forward to going home. It's so lonely now."

"Surely no lonelier than it's been for the last couple of years."

"Somehow, Roscoe's being back among the living makes me feel lonelier. I know that doesn't make sense, but it's how I feel. And think how Alvin must feel, all alone in that house of his, an absent wife, and a brother waiting outside to kill him."

"He's alone? Didn't he call those security people I recommended?"

"That's all arranged. They're watching the outside of the house. They're hoping to trap Roscoe, though they promised not to hurt him."

I grunted. I hoped they planned to keep their promise. "Let's go." I stood up, escorted Rita to the cash register, paid the bill, and took her out to my car. "I'll drop you off home."

"I would hope so. Maybe you can come in for a minute. I'd like you to walk through the house with me, help me look in the closets and under the beds. It'd make me feel better."

"You don't think Roscoe's after you, do you?"

"No, he'd never hurt me, even if he isn't in his right mind. But I still feel vulnerable. A little scared, in fact."

I couldn't think of any good reason to turn her down, and it was probably a good idea. "Don't worry, I'll help shake down the place for you, but I'm sure we won't find anything more dangerous than dust bunnies."

15

On the drive to her house Rita was uncharacteristically quiet. I was sure she was worried about Alvin, but it sounded like he was in good hands. When we got there, we searched the whole house together, turning lights on in every room, looking in closets, behind drapes, and under the beds. In Rita's bedroom her nightgown was lying across the bedspread, black and lacy and not very substantial. That was the scariest thing in the room. We made the whole circuit and ended up back in the living room.

"We're alone," I told her, but I didn't mean it to sound like it did. She gave me a look like a guy likes to get, but I figured I was the wrong guy. "I've got to go."

"Just stay another minute, please. I'd offer you coffee, but you're probably sloshing already." The phone rang. "Don't go, it might be Alvin."

I found a chair and sat down.

Rita was on the phone for quite a while. I

watched her while she stood by the little phone table and talked. There was a comfortable-looking chair right by her elbow, but she didn't sit down. After the first couple of minutes I got bored and nosey and started to eavesdrop in earnest.

Listening in on a phone conversation is always a challenge because you can only hear one side of the conversation you have to guess at the part you can't hear. The tendency is to get a bit too creative and start handing the invisible talker all the wrong lines.

I established fairly early that the caller wasn't Alvin, but it was somebody Rita knew fairly well. A man, though a hysterical one.

"If that's who you say it was, I believe you." Rita was using her patient voice. "I'm sure you would know if it was simply a practical joke. No, I certainly don't consider you an idiot." Then silence while she listened. "Call it whatever you want. Woman's intuition will do. I have my reasons, but I don't feel like talking about it. And it doesn't matter what the police say."

That pricked up my ears. Mention of the cops always does that to me.

"They're doing their job as they see fit. They've taken your statement and they'll keep an eye out." She paused. "They'll send a patrol car through your neighborhood now and then. That's all you can expect from them. Milton, don't take it personally. It has nothing to do with your being an — artist. Do they even know?"

Milton? How did that boy get tangled up with the cops? And here I was thinking it might have been something important. I stood up, reached for my hat lying on the arm of the chair. I waved goodbye to Rita and her eyes went wide. She put her free hand over the receiver and whispered at me fiercely: "Don't go. It's about Roscoe. He's called Milton and threatened to kill him too. You have to stay. Please."

I sat back down. Why would Roscoe want to kill Milton? Jealousy? That made no sense, not with Milton. But if Roscoe was really crazy, and I had no reason to believe otherwise, then his behavior didn't have to make sense. The whole situation was getting crazy, and it was no longer confined to just the Ravencamp family. I heard Rita mention my name.

"No, not on a professional level. We're friends. We just returned from having dinner. Axe drove me home. Anyway, he's here. Would you like to talk to him? He might be able to give you some advice." She placed her hand over the receiver again. "He wants to talk to you."

I stood up and grudgingly took the phone. "Yeah? This is Axe Hatchett. What gives?"

"So surly! I didn't even want to talk to you. It was Rita's idea. I certainly didn't intend to ruin the remainder of your romantic evening."

I decided I could really learn to dislike this guy. "Rita tells me her dead husband just called you and threatened to kill you. Is that true?"

"Excuse me. Rita's husband. He is clearly not deceased. First he threatens to kill his own brother, and now me, an old friend. Maybe he'll kill us both while you and the police stand by and do your nails, or whatever."

"Don't mention me and the cops in the same sentence, Milton. Alvin's OK. He's being guarded. You shouldn't have loaned him your gun. Now what are you going to do? Do you have any other guns?"

Milton's voice had become suddenly quiet and polite. Almost respectful. "Actually, Mr. Hatchett, I was hoping you would come protect me. Rita says that's a possibility. I'd pay your usual fee, plus a bonus. I would greatly appreciate it. And, truthfully, wouldn't you feel guilty if I was horribly murdered because you had refused to help?"

"I'd have to think about it. Listen, I gather you aren't too happy about the way the police are handling your complaint."

"My complaint? You make it sound so insignificant. But then, that's how the police are treating it. If I leave them to handle it, I'll be dead by tomorrow."

"Did Roscoe say he was going to kill you tonight?"

"No, he didn't specify the time. If I am still alive tomorrow, I intend to hire an entire crew of stalwart protectors, heavily armed. But what am I to do tonight?"

I thought about it. What the hell? I could spend

the night watching out for the guy. As long as he didn't try talking to me. "All right, I'll do it. But I'll need to stop off at my place and pick up an extra gun. All I've got on me is my little thirty-eight."

"Where do you live?"

I told him.

"That's quite a distance from my place. Rita's, on the other hand, is quite close to me. Maybe you can borrow one of Roscoe's guns from her. He owned several."

"I'll talk to her about it. Give me your address and phone number, and directions, and I'll get over to your place as soon as I can. I'll call you when I'm ready to start."

"Thank you so much! You're a life saver, literally."

"Don't overdo it."

He gave me the information I'd asked for and I hung up the phone. I turned to Rita. "Looks like I'll be babysitting Milton tonight. He says you might have a gun or two I might borrow."

"Roscoe's? Yes, I suppose. They're in Roscoe's den in the basement. I'll show you where they are. Thank you for agreeing to watch Milton. He's very upset, and scared."

I'd already seen Roscoe's den once when we'd gone through the house looking for monsters in the closets. It was a dark-paneled, low-ceilinged room with a brick fireplace and built-in shelves along a couple of the walls. I hadn't noticed a gun rack, but there was one, hidden behind one of two hinged mirrors that decorated each side of the fireplace.

There were five guns, three rifles, and two shotguns. One of the rifles was a fancy .30-06, a deer gun, with a high-power scope and a custom stock. I didn't need it to protect Milton. Instead, I selected a nice Twelve-gauge pump shotgun. I found a box of shells in a drawer beneath the mirror. I was ready to go, so Rita and I headed back upstairs.

"Be careful," she told me as I opened her door. "Call me when you get there. And let me know if anything...happens."

"Nothing's going to happen. It's going to be just like babysitting Alvin. Just a long night of no sleep."

"I hope that proves true."

"Don't be so glum. Everything will be fine. I'll see you around."

"Is Roscoe's gun loaded?"

"It will be. Stop worrying, Mom. I've got my galoshes on. Did you remember to pack a cupcake in my lunch?"

"Don't make jokes. I want you to be careful."

"I'm always careful. It's the code of the coward. Cheer up. Someday we'll look back on all this, if we're still alive, and laugh."

Milton's place turned out to be about the same distance from Rita's as it was from Alvin's, though a little north of both of them. I followed a winding dirt road that wove along a creek bed. The property taxes were pretty low in this neighborhood because every decade or so the creek jumped its banks and filled people's living rooms with mud and snakes.

Like many of the area's houses, Milton's was guarded by a three-foot-high wall made of concrete blocks. This was supposed to keep the creek from inviting itself into folks' yards and I hoped it worked. The house was one story, smallish, with a garage so narrow I wondered how Milton managed to squeeze his big Roadmaster into it. On the south side of the house, some kind of greenhouse-looking structure had been added. I gathered this was Milton's artist studio.

The house was lit up like a jack-o-lantern, every window illuminated, the light filtered through the closed curtains. I parked the Hudson outside the retaining wall and walked through the open gate to the front door. I kept an eye out the whole time for lurking figures in the darkness that might, or might not, be Roscoe.

A tall oval of etched glass filled up a good part of the front door, and there was a thin curtain behind it that twitched a little as I stepped onto the porch. Roscoe's shotgun dangled from my left hand. There was no bell so I knocked.

The door creaked open just enough to let a butterfly enter if it squeezed in sideways.

"Yes?" challenged a ridiculously low voice. Milton, trying to be a baritone.

"Rita sent me. I've got the pickles if you've got the penguin."

"What?"

"Did I get the password wrong? Come on, Milton, let me in. I'm obviously not Roscoe."

The door opened a little more and I slid through it, wishing I hadn't eaten so much for dinner. Milton closed and bolted the door before I could even get my hat off. He turned toward me. "You're armed."

I raised the shotgun "I also have my Chiefs snub-nose."

"That's all?"

"No, I'm carrying a grenade launcher in an ankle holster, but I won't show it to you because my socks are dirty."

"Levity. At a time like this."

"There's always time for levity."

I looked around. We were in a small living room. Knotty-pine paneling, shiny oak floors showing around the edges of a dark-patterned carpet. Worn but comfortable-looking overstuffed furniture—a couch and two chairs. There was also a rocking chair and an old-fashioned floor lamp with a fringed shade. All the place needed was starched doilies and it would have been ready for my grandma to move into.

There was a fire burning in the river stone fireplace though it was not cold out. Maybe Milton thought Roscoe might try to come down the chimney like Santa, only armed.

"Please be seated," said Milton. "I recommend the sofa for comfort. Can I get you anything? Coffee?"

"Maybe later, thanks." When I sat down on the couch I noticed a fancy box on the coffee table. It looked like something a good bottle of liquor would come in. "A birthday present?"

"No, just a gift. From a secret admirer, apparently. Someone left it at Rita's shop for me — somebody she didn't recognize. I teach a painting class for a small group of people. Maybe one of them likes me better than I realized. God knows, I don't like any of them. If it wasn't for their money — "

"Why don't you open it? It might cheer you up."

"I suppose I should open it, but the box is so pretty. I'll be disappointed if the gift isn't also special."

"Go on, open it."

He picked up the box and started fussing with the tape on the silver-and-red wrapping paper. It was awfully slow going. "I don't want to tear it," he explained. "I always save wrapping paper. Such a waste not to."

"Sure, it pays to be frugal. When I do my laundry I save the dryer lint to make pillows out of. You know, for Christmas presents."

"I sincerely hope my secret admirer isn't as frugal, or gauche, as you." He finally got the paper off, which he carefully folded, then he opened the top flap of the cardboard box he'd uncovered. He pulled out a bottle. No surprise there. The bottle was dark and dusty. "My word," Milton said, giving the bottle a good looking over, "a bottle of fifty-year-old brandy. Imagine. This had to cost a pretty penny! I'm impressed. This calls for a celebration. Can I offer you a glass?"

"I appreciate the offer, but no thanks. I need to keep my mind clear in case Roscoe shows up."

"Well, since you're here to protect me now, I guess I can drink as much as I want."

"Fine, but I'd rather you didn't get too sloshed. Drunks don't make very good company."

"I can assure you I won't be imbibing to that extent."

He left the room, passing through a doorway into what I would soon discover was a small dining room. I heard a door squeak, possibly on a china cupboard, and a moment later Milton returned with a bulbous brandy snifter.

He held it up to the light, checking for dust, then set it on the coffee table. After he poured a generous snort into his glass, he took an appreciative sniff at the contents. It had a lovely amber color and I could smell the stuff from my perch on the couch.

"Smells like the real thing," I said.

"Ah, yes. Sure you don't want a taste? Surely a little won't hurt your bulldog vigilance."

"You can never be too careful. Have one for me."

He swirled the hooch around in his glass and took another long sniff, then set it on the fireplace mantle untasted. He returned to the coffee table and opened the lid of an ornate gold box that could have served as a coffin for some member of hamster royalty. He fingered out a cigarette, short, cork tipped, with a gold band around the end you light.

The open box smelled of perfume, but also of some pretty strong Turkish tobacco. He picked up a gold table lighter about the size of a grenade and set fire to the prissy cigarette.

"Say, do you mind if I smoke a cigar? It's been a few hours."

"I'd sooner you set fire to a stack of tractor tires in my living room."

"Oh? Not an appreciator of cigars, huh?"

"Hardly. Besides, I can imagine what kind of cigars you smoke. Big, fat, black ones, with showy cigar bands. And instead of clipping off the ends with a guillotine cutter, you likely bite them off with your teeth and spit the dross on the floor. No doubt you also light them by lifting your thigh and scratching a kitchen match on the stretched fabric of your trousers."

"Yeah, so?"

"Why not enjoy one of my fine cigarettes?" He gestured at the open gold box.

I dug one out and sniffed it. "Do I light this, or eat it for dessert?"

"The tobacco is excellent."

I lit the thing with the table lighter and took a drag. It wasn't bad. I figured I wouldn't turn into a swish like Milton just by smoking one of his prissy cigarettes, but I sure wasn't going to risk smoking a second one. "You're right, it's swell tobacco."

Milton smiled, then shifted a little in his chair by the fireplace. He lifted his snifter off the mantle, swirled the brandy around, and took an experimental sip. "Amazing." He took a bigger sip, then another. "Why can't all brandy be fifty years old?"

"I guess it could be if people stopped drinking it straight from the still."

He tilted the glass and emptied it. "Just one more." He poured out a slightly larger drink this time. I was hoping this wouldn't be the second night in a row I had to spend with a drunk.

16

"So, what exactly did Roscoe say to you when he called?"

Milton almost choked. "Must you remind me?"

"You mean you'd forgotten? Come on, what'd he say? It's the kind of information I might be able to use to help you and Alvin both."

He took a big slug of brandy without bothering to swirl it this time. I noticed that his eyelids were beginning to droop. Either Milton really couldn't hold his liquor, or something else was going on.

I considered the possibilities. Maybe fifty-year-old brandy was stronger than the younger stuff. I wouldn't know. Or maybe Milton had been drinking before I arrived. Or, and this idea really bothered me, the brandy might be doped. What if Milton's secret admirer was Roscoe? I was glad I hadn't partaken of the stuff.

"Slow down on the drinking, OK? I need to talk to you."

"Don't worry, I won't get too drunk to talk. In

fact, I think you'll find my tongue will be pleasant-
ly loose." He emptied the snifter, poured out some
more, settled deeper in his chair. "You want to
know why Roscoe would want to kill me and Alvin?"

"Yeah, I'd be interested." I stubbed out the remains of my cigarette in a glass ashtray shaped
like a sitting bird, maybe a quail.

"Illicit love, and blackmail. I'd beg you to keep
all this to yourself, but I know you won't say anything. You love Rita too much. Men find Rita hard
to resist, especially men like you."

"OK, I'll bite. What kind of man am I?"

"Rough, brutal, violent, demanding, thick-
headed."

"Hey, that's just what my mom's always said
about me."

"You're like Roscoe. Poor, jealous, possessive
Roscoe. How could anyone know he wasn't dead?
I certainly don't blame Rita for seeking romance.
She's a fiery young woman. But she shouldn't
have taken up with Alvin, a married man. I don't
care that Roscoe was his brother, what difference
should that make? But it wasn't right to cheat on
Della, was it? I'm sorry. You don't know who Della is. That's Alvin's estranged wife. "

"I've heard something about her, as well as Alvin and Rita's affair."

Milton raised his eyebrows at me. He fished
another cigarette out of the box and lit it, all a bit
clumsily. "Have another one. Please."

I took another one and set fire to it. What the hell. If I turned into a swish, it might at least improve my cooking.

"I found out about the affair by accident. I was disappointed in them both. They were my friends, had been since grade school. I decided to punish them."

"By blackmailing them. Is that why you did it? It didn't have anything to do with the money you squeezed out of them?"

"Think what you like." He took a sip of hooch. He was drinking more slowly now. "I admit I wanted the money. I'd been fired from my job at the high school. A horrid job teaching talentless teenagers to waste paint and clay. I made the mistake of pointing out to one of my students, though quite accurately, that her attempt at a recreation of a Grecian urn looked more like the unsuccessful prototype of a toilet. Unfortunately for me, the girl had a close relative working in the administration building. I was relieved of my duties. I felt relieved, too, until payday."

"So, you followed Rita and Alvin around and took snapshots of them mating in a motel room, or wherever."

"In a meadow, actually. I sent copies of the photos to them with my demand for what I considered a reasonable amount of money to not send the pictures to Della. I made a couple of more requests for money, but then somehow Rita and Alvin figured out I was the blackmailer. I thought

Alvin was going to kill me, but I promised to turn over all of the pictures I had, and the negatives, and start paying back the blackmail money as soon as conveniently possible. And now Roscoe wants to kill me." He stopped talking and his eyes got very big. He'd heard something.

Me too. It was the crunching of gravel as somebody drove slowly by the house. I got up and went to the front door where I'd leaned Roscoe's shotgun. I peeked around the curtain that covered the oval glass in the door. I saw the headlights of a car that was apparently turning around in front of the house. In a moment it disappeared down the road. "False alarm." I turned back to Milton. He was standing up, and his face had turned pale.

"I want you to go through my house and make sure everything's locked up and safe. Doors, windows, the attic and cellar doors. I'll go with you."

So, for the second time that night, I looked through closets, under beds, behind curtains, anywhere a guy the size of Roscoe could hide. Milton's bedroom had a pair of old French doors that seemed none too secure. I told him he'd have to sleep someplace else that night. I also noticed a faint scent of perfume around Milton's double bed. Lady's perfume. Perhaps I was wrong about the guy's inclinations. It's hard to tell with those artist types.

We finished our inspection in the greenhouse I'd noticed when I drove up to the place. I'd been right, it was Milton's studio. Considering how neat the rest of the house was, I was surprised at the mess that greeted us in the studio. The place was a cluttered dump. There were easels covered with paint-spattered sheets, unfinished sculptures, and a long table strewn with half-squeezed paint tubes, cans of turpentine and linseed oil, dirty brushes sticking out of containers of oily liquids. There was a workbench with a few tools scattered on it.

Milton looked over the assortment and picked up what looked like a sledgehammer with a very short handle. He handed it to me, then started pawing through some little drawers until he came up with a handful of mismatched nails, some of them bent or with the heads damaged. He dropped them into my palm.

"Will any of these work for nailing my cellar trap door shut?"

"Is that what you want?" We'd already been down in the little windowless cellar and the trapdoor was in the floor of a little pantry right off the kitchen. "I don't think anybody can get into your cellar from outside, but if you want me to seal the door shut, I will. I guess some of these nails will work."

"Those are all I have. I'm not a carpenter you know."

"I realize that. You're more of an arts and crafts kind of guy. "

He gave me a look that would have killed a less hardy man. "Arts and crafts are for old maids and bored housewives. I'm an artist. Please be kind enough to make the distinction."

"I'll make the effort."

He looked over at the workbench, then suddenly grabbed a little dustpan and broom. I thought he was going to attack me with them, but instead he swept up a tiny pile of debris on the bench top and emptied it into an otherwise empty metal trash basket. I hoped it made him feel better. He then led me around the studio and I checked all the horizontally-hinged windows and the metal door that led outside.

Everything was latched and locked. I didn't think it would take much to break into the place, but you couldn't do it without making a bunch of noise. Satisfied, I had Milton lead me back into the main part of the house. While I secured the trapdoor with a couple of well-placed ten-penny nails, I had Milton make coffee for me. He was banging things around a little, and I hoped the brandy was starting to wear off.

"I've got the door nailed down for you," I hollered to him. "I'll put the hammer and the rest of the nails back in your greenhouse. OK?"

"Studio. Your coffee's almost done. Let me guess, black?"

"You got it."

I headed for the studio, which I accessed using a door located just off the little dining room. I put the hammer back on the bench and stuck the remaining nails in one of the little drawers, then I did what I'd actually come to do: I picked up the waste basket and sorted through its contents to see what Milton wanted to hide from me.

There wasn't much there. Some sawdust and metal filings, a few bent brads of the type used to fasten canvases to frames, an empty tube of glue, and a little cone of metal, maybe steel. The fat end of the cone was wedge-shaped, like it'd been cut with a wire cutters, or a pair of dikes. It was the only interesting thing in the whole mess. There was something vaguely familiar about it.

I keep a couple of small envelopes on me most of the time, the kind that hold baby announcements and crap like that. I use them to collect evidence. I took one out of my pocket now, a pink one, and dropped the cone of metal in it, sealed the envelope, and dropped it back in my pocket. Then I went back to the living room.

"Get lost?" Milton asked when I took my place back on the couch. There was a big crockery mug on the coffee table, on a coaster, with a folded paper napkin next to it. A napkin for a cup of coffee?

"I thought I heard something out in your backyard. I went out your studio door to check it out. I didn't find anything. It was probably just the wind."

"I sincerely hope you're correct."

Milton had returned to his chair by the fireplace, and had even thrown a couple of logs on, though the room was already hot and stuffy. He was smoking another cigarette, and I was sorry to see he'd poured himself another generous brandy. He drank about half of it while I watched in disgust. It was going to be a long night. There was a pleasant silence for a few moments, and then he began talking. His words weren't slurred yet, but he was getting there. "I take it you were in the military, in the war."

"That's right."

"A war hero?"

"Not so you'd notice. And you?"

"No. I was born with an enlarged spleen. I received a medical deferment, but I still managed to help in the war effort. I moved to Los Angeles for the duration of the conflict, and I was fortunate enough to receive a grant to finance the making of a series of films I submitted to the War Department. One of my films was selected and shown to troops throughout the country."

"Oh, yeah? Maybe I saw it. What was it about?"

"It was a hygiene film, concerning the importance of practicing sanitary urination. If I told you the names of the actors who appeared in my film, I think you'd be impressed. They, too, wanted to contribute to the war effort and they actually worked for free."

"Famous guys?"

"Pretty well known, yes."

"Come on, who were they? Let me guess. Betty Grable and Franchot Tone?"

"Don't be ridiculous. What would you say to Coleman Hart and Dirk Binner?"

"Pretty heavy hitters. I just saw Dirk Binner's newest pirate film. Did you write this movie, or direct it, or what?"

"It was hardly a movie. It was a short. And I didn't write it. The fellow who wrote the screen play for 'Pinocchio' was responsible. At least, that was the rumor at the time."

"Offhand I can't recall seeing it, but I may have been stuck doing KP. Tell me about it. What was the plot?"

"Well, it was only a few minutes long. I don't know if you'd say it had a plot, exactly." He emptied his snifter again. "Mind if I have another?"

"It's your place, your bottle."

He clumsily left his chair, poured another brandy, lit another cigarette. "Help yourself," he said, waving a hand at the gold box. I took another one and set fire to it. He returned to his chair.

"Hart did a good job. Binner was a bit nervous, poor man. We did the filming in an actual men's room to provide authenticity. There was a lot of shiny tile on the walls that the urinals were attached to. They played hell with the lighting, and the place was like an echo chamber. The actors had to practically whisper to keep their words from echoing. It gave the film an odd, conspiratorial quality, which I rather liked.

"Coleman Hart had the first line. He turns to Binner, who's standing at the urinal next to him, and says, 'Try hitting the urinal, why can't you? There's a war on you know.' Binner just snickers.

'What's this war got to do with latrines? It's about winning, that's the only thing that matters'

"Hart says 'Think so, Private? Listen, if you can't be trusted to hit the bull's-eye when you're taking a leak, who's going to trust you behind a set of gun sights? You could end up killing your own troops. You ever think of that? Not to mention, piddling on the floor's a filthy habit. It encourages disease. How'd you feel if your entire unit came down with something because of you? What if they couldn't fight? What if we lost this war because of your sloppiness, Private?'

"Dirk Binner hangs his head, you can hear him shuffling his feet, and when he speaks again you can tell there's a lump in his throat. 'Gosh, I'm sorry, I feel like a heel. Worse, I feel like a bad soldier. I didn't mean anything by missing the urinal, honest. I was just being careless. But it won't happen again. You put me straight, and I won't forget it. I know you're just another private, like me, but you just taught me something important. I want you to know you don't have to worry about putting me behind a set of gun sights. From now on I'll be on target whether I'm on the battlefield or right here in the latrine.'"

I almost felt like applauding. Almost. "Say, why didn't you continue with your movie career? Why'd you move back here?"

Milton made a vague gesture in the air with the hand that wasn't holding the brandy glass. "I was born and raised in Quartz Quarry. I couldn't stay away, somehow. But I do sometimes wonder what I could have become if I'd stayed in LA, and stayed in the movie business."

I drank my coffee, which was pretty good. I stepped into the kitchen and poured a second cup, then returned to my place on the couch. I drank coffee while Milton continued to snort his ancient hooch. I was getting bored and a little sleepy. "How's about a game of checkers?"

"I don't own any."

"No? What kind of cards do you play? Crazy Eights? Animal Rummy?"

"I don't play cards. I don't believe in gambling."

There was a big console radio against one wall. "How about some music? We can keep it turned down low so we can hear if someone starts creeping around the house outside."

"Well, I suppose some music might be all right. I wish I could get a classical station in this benighted city."

"I was thinking of something a little more modern. Something I could actually listen to without gritting my teeth."

Milton walked carefully over to the radio, fired it up, and in a couple of minutes Frank Sinatra was crooning about the wee small hours of the morning.

"That's better," I said. "It'll take your mind off of you-know-who."

"You mean Roscoe. Roscoe the killer." He refreshed his drink.

"Isn't that bottle about empty?"

"Fortunately, no. Roscoe the killer."

"You really think he'll kill you? Or Alvin? You knew him most of your life. Surely he can't have changed that much."

"He doesn't have to have changed. He's been a killer for years."

"What do you mean? I know he was a sniper in the war, but that's all over with."

Milton gave me a bleary-eyed, incredulous look. "I assumed you knew. I can't imagine that Rita or Alvin didn't tell you. I mean, they've hired you to track the madman down. Didn't they warn you?"

"About what? I mean, I know Roscoe has a gun, a pistol, if that's what you're talking about." A strange queasiness hit me in the gut, and I didn't think it had anything to do with the meal I'd had at Italo's. "Maybe I should call Alvin and ask him about it. Can I borrow your phone?"

"You may, but he won't answer. Orders from the security thugs he hired. All the better to trap Roscoe. Rita apprised me of the situation earlier today."

I thought I'd recommended a reliable security agency, but now I was beginning to wonder. "Well, maybe I should call Rita."

"Do you never tire of her? I can tell you everything you need to know about Roscoe, and what I say will be the truth."

I doubted that, but I was still curious about what he might have to say. "All right, tell me your bedtime story."

"Gladly. But, where to start...where to start?"

17

Milton swirled the brandy in his glass and sloshed a little on his shirt. "Most of this story I have from Alvin. Apparently, while sniping in the jungles during the war, Roscoe developed a taste for killing. A thirst, you might say. On returning to civilian life he discovered that the killing of wild animals, during his hunting expeditions, did not satisfy him any longer. So he began shooting his fellow hunters. I probably shouldn't be telling you this."

"Nonsense. Have another drink, tell me the rest of the story."

"It could have been the death of his father in a hunting accident that set him off; turned him into a rogue, so to speak. It's impossible to know how many unfortunate deer hunters lost their lives to Roscoe's rifle. However, Alvin figured out what was going on. You see, after the death of Gus Ravencamp, Alvin gave up hunting, so Roscoe began going alone. But even though he had always been a successful hunter in the past, he began returning from his annual hunting trips with nothing to show for it. No venison for the freezer. His lack of success didn't appear to bother him much. And, interestingly, tragic hunting accidents began to occur with alarming frequency.

"For a time, each deer-hunting season was punctuated by the shooting death of some unfortunate sportsman. Alvin began collecting the newspaper articles concerning these deaths. The chilling truth was that the hunters were shot, generally in the back, at the very times when Roscoe was away on his own hunting excursions. Not only that, but they happened in those parts of the mountains where Roscoe chose to hunt."

"Could be coincidence. Alvin never had any proof, did he?"

"Well. Actually.... You know, I do believe I might have had one too many brandies. Assuming that I survive this night, I may wish I was dead in the morning. Do you get hangovers, Mr. Hatchett?"

"Who cares if I get hangovers? Get on with your story. This is important stuff if it's true."

"But the tale can wait. I believe, if you'll excuse me, that I might take a little nap."

"Like hell you will. Drink some coffee. Step outside and get some air. Think of Roscoe. Maybe he's outside right now waiting for you to nod off so he can come in and riddle you full of lead."

"You'll protect me."

"Don't count on it. What if I fall asleep too?'

"You won't. I have complete confidence in you."

And while I watched, the idiot went and fell asleep right there in his chair. Now all I had for company was Nat King Cole warbling about Gypsies, and blossoms falling. The phone rang. Milton jumped about three feet in the air, both his mouth and his eyes wide open. But he didn't move to answer the phone.

After the forth ring I jumped up and started yelling at him: "Answer the damn thing!"

He was still frozen in his chair. "I can't. What if it's him? You answer."

"I can't, I don't want him to know I'm here." The phone kept ringing and Milton refused to move. I grabbed it on the tenth ring. "Yeah? Who is this?"

"Is that you, Axe? It's me, Alvin. Where's Milton?"

"He's feeling a little under the weather. Can I take a message?"

"Huh? No, it's nothing important, I was just checking up on him. Things are all right over there? Why are you at Milton's?"

"Everything's lovely over here. I guess you haven't heard the news. Roscoe called Milton and threatened to kill him. Say, I just thought of something. If you're not supposed to answer the phone, what happens when Della calls?"

"I'm not sure. I called her myself tonight and

tried to explain things to her. Can you believe it? She thinks I'm making up all this stuff about Roscoe! That's Della for you. Roscoe called Milton? When?"

"Maybe she'll believe you if Roscoe kills you. Some people just need a lot of convincing. I don't know when your brother called Milton. A couple of hours ago, maybe. Say, what's this I hear about your brother getting a little confused on his hunting trips? Do you really believe he killed a bunch of hunters?"

There was silence on the other end of the line so long I thought maybe the connection had been broken. "You weren't supposed to know that," he said, finally. "Who told you that? It couldn't have been Rita."

"It doesn't matter who told me. You should have told me yourself. Didn't you think it was something I ought to know? How many other things have you kept from me?"

"Nothing important, I swear. Listen, that stuff about Roscoe, about his shooting hunters, nobody can prove that. And it's kind of a family secret, if you know what I mean. I'd appreciate it if you kept it under your hat."

"My hat's not for keeping secrets, it's to keep my head covered. Does Della know about this family secret of yours?"

"Of course. Why?"

"No reason. Give me a call in the morning if you're still alive, will you? I'll likely still be here, babysitting Milton."

"Sure thing. I hope we all make it through the night."

I hung up, turned off the radio, and shook Milton who had fallen asleep again. He didn't wake up, but at least he stopped snoring. I had a lot of things to think about, and I needed quiet. But just as I was trying to put two and two together, the damn phone started ringing again. Milton woke up, so I grabbed the receiver and stuck it in his hand. "Say 'hello,'" I told him.

"Hello? Oh, it's you. I was afraid it was him. No, it's been a quiet night so far. Guess what my little gift from work turned out to be?" He paused. "No" He paused again. "No, not that either. What? It wouldn't even fit in a box that size. I'll tell you. A lovely bottle of brandy. Fifty-years-old. I've already had a sip of it. No, he insists that he's on duty, and maybe it's a good idea. Alvin? Yes, I think he just called here. Mr. Hatchett talked to him. Would you like to speak with your detective?"

I was waving my arms at Milton like a bull-fighter, trying to make him understand I didn't want to talk to Rita. I was sure it was her on the phone. But Milton either didn't understand my sign language, or was just perverse enough to pretend he didn't get my message. He held the receiver out to me. "It's your Rita. She misses you and wants to talk to you."

I grudgingly took the phone. "Yeah? It's you

again, huh? "

"You sound disappointed. I hope Milton's not annoying you, I know how he can be sometimes. Are the two of you getting along?"

"Sure, we're pals. There's been no sign of your husband yet. Maybe he's decided to kill Alvin first. Or perhaps he's calling somebody else and threatening to shoot him. You haven't heard from him, have you?"

"No, thank God. I'm not sure what I'd do if he called me. I don't know if I'd be able to talk to him. I just wish all of this was over with. Tell me things will be OK, that everything will work out. I promise to believe you."

"If I told you that, even I wouldn't believe me. Listen, Milton talks in his sleep. What's this about your missing husband sniping unsuspecting deer hunters? Any truth to that? Alvin tells me it's all hush-hush and should be kept in the family, but I have a feeling the families of those dead hunters might not agree. What's your position?"

"My God! I can't believe Milton told you about that. He shouldn't even know about those things himself. It should have been kept in the family! That's my fault, and I feel betrayed."

"Ah, you can't be too hard on the guy, he has a lot of brandy in him, and it loosened his tongue. Anyway, what do you know about it?"

"Nothing much. Alvin's the one who knows the most about it. Unfortunately, he kept Roscoe's little secret to himself for a long time. Years. By the time he got around to telling me and Ethel and Della, Roscoe had likely shot several hunters. Alvin kept a scrapbook of newspaper clippings. A scrapbook, like it was some kind of hobby! I can understand why he had a hard time figuring out what to do, and it's doubtful the murders can ever be proven. They weren't investigated as murders, but as accidents. Still, Alvin should have told the rest of us much sooner."

"I'm curious, did Alvin, or any of you, confront Roscoe with his crimes?"

"Alvin claims to have had it out with Roscoe, but I'm not sure if he really had the courage to do that. Anyway, according to Alvin, Roscoe admitted to the killings and then dared his brother to do something about it."

"But you never said anything to your husband? Never let him know you were aware of his tastes in wild game?"

"No, and I feel bad about it. I just suggested that Alvin's a coward, but maybe I should have kept that description for me. I was afraid to say anything to him, even though I'm pretty sure he realized Alvin had told me all he knew."

"You said Alvin told his mom? That must have been pretty hard on her. If she believed Alvin, then she must have thought Roscoe was a murderer. But if she didn't buy Alvin's story, then she must have thought Alvin was crazy. There was no good way for her to take that kind of news."

"I thought his telling her was a mistake, and

pretty damned insensitive." There was an angry edge to her voice that I hadn't heard before.

"OK, just a couple more questions."

"Will the answers to these questions help you keep my husband alive? Will they help in capturing him and keeping him safe so that he can get the medical treatment he needs?"

"Actually, no. Forget the questions. I think we're through talking. Do you want me to put Milton back on the horn?"

"No, I was only checking up. I'm sorry I got mad. We should have told you the whole story right at the beginning, but sometimes it's hard to give away secrets."

"Sure, sure, don't worry about it. So long."

"Goodbye."

I hung up the phone with a little more force than was necessary. Milton jumped. What a nice little den of snakes I was in the middle of. I felt I needed some air, and a cigar. I moved to the front door and picked up the pump shotgun I'd borrowed from Rita. Milton raised his eyebrows, started to get up from his chair. "Stay here," I told him. "I'm going to take a walk around outside. I just want to take a look and make sure everything's OK. I'll be back in a few minutes."

"Don't take too long, please."

"Don't worry. Have another shot of brandy."

"Knock three times, slowly, when you want back in."

Once outside, I found that the temperature had

dropped and there was a fine rain falling. I would have cursed the rain, but I realized it actually felt pretty good. I chewed the end off a cigar, lit a match with my thumbnail, and managed to grow a coal on the business end of my cigar before the rain could put it out.

I took a slow walk around the inside perimeter of the concrete block wall. There were some bushes and trees, and I checked them out to make sure no murderers were taking refuge in them. Once I'd walked around the entire yard, I checked the house itself, looking at the windows and doors and making sure they were secured. And after that, I just stood around in the drizzle, the shotgun in the crook of my arm, and did some smoking and some thinking.

I was mad, of course. I'd been hired to find a guy who I'd been told might have amnesia and a gun. Now I'd learned he had possibly murdered several hunters, and yet at no time, and in no way, had I been warned about the amount of danger I was in while I was tracking down Roscoe Ravencamp. I wondered what Rita and Alvin had told the cops. The same as they'd told me? Probably.

Then I realized it didn't matter because I still didn't believe Rita's husband had come back from the dead. It was a hoax. But what was the purpose of the hoax? I needed to figure that out. Why was I being led to believe that the resurrected Roscoe had threatened to shoot both his brother and an old friend? What was the point?

There were a couple of things kicking around in the back of my mind that wouldn't leave me alone. There was something that I should have figured out, some clue that I knew about but wasn't using. However, I decided to go back inside.

When I came in the front door, Milton greeted me by pointing a little pistol at me.

"Sorry," he told me, putting the pint-sized pearl-handled gun in his pocket. "I didn't know it was you. We agreed you'd knock three times, slowly."

I gave him what must have been a sheepish smile. "You're right, I forgot. If you'd shot me, I couldn't have blamed you. Say, how many guns do you own anyway?"

"Just this one."

"What about the one you loaned Alvin?"

"Well, yes, that one too." He made a face. "You've been smoking a cigar, I can smell it on your clothes."

"Sorry. I like the smell myself."

"Well, for me it's hardly perfume."

I had taken my hat off and was preparing to resume sentry duty on the couch when the two clues that had been lurking in the basement of my brain decided to come upstairs and tell me a thing or two. "Get your hat on, Milton, we're going. And grab your coat. It's raining."

The eyes he showed me belonged to a frightened rabbit. "What do you mean, my hat?"

"We're going out. We're taking a little drive, and it's going to be a fast one." He didn't move, so I stepped forward and grabbed him by the shoulder and pushed him out the front door.

"What is this? How dare you!"

His hat was on a tiny table near the door. I put it on his head, backwards, and headed us both into the yard and toward my car.

"Wait," he said, "I need to lock up."

"No you don't. The only dangerous person in this neighborhood is you, and you're going with me." I shoved him into the passenger's side of the Hornet and got in on the driver's side. I'd figured some things out and I only hoped it wasn't too late.

18

The Hudson's always had plenty under the hood, and I know a mechanic who I think dabbles in the dark arts — it's the fastest thing on four tires I've ever had the pleasure of piloting. Of course, I couldn't drive flat out on this curvy dirt road, but I was making pretty good time. Every time I took a hard right, Milton slammed up against the door. And every time I took a hard left, he practically slid into my lap.

"Where are we going, where are you taking me?" His teeth were almost chattering with fear.

"You'll see. I just hope we aren't going to the scene of a murder." I realized at that moment that I should have taken time to call the cops before we left Milton's. Well, if I was lucky, I could run a couple of red lights in town at high speed and attract a patrol car or two. It wasn't likely, though. It was late enough at night that the good citizens of Quartz Quarry were either huddled in front of their televisions or in their beds.

"I insist you stop this car and let me out," Milton said in the voice he probably used on his pupils when he'd still been teaching art in high school.

"You can get out if you want, but I'm not stopping, or slowing down. By the way, I want that pea shooter of yours. Hand it over."

"Pea shooter? What?"

"The gun. The one that's in your pocket. Hand it over, and don't try anything fancy."

"I don't have it, I swear. I took it out of my pocket when we left the house. I was afraid. I dropped it. We can go back for it."

He was lying. I knew the pistol was still in his pocket, but there wasn't much I could do until I stopped the car. I just had to keep an eye on him. "That old revolver of yours that you loaned to Alvin, why didn't you give him all of it?"

"What? What nonsense are you spouting now?"

"That little bit of steel you so tidily swept into the dust bin when we were in your studio. It was the last quarter-inch or so of the firing pin on that old Peacemaker you let Alvin borrow. You must have touched-up the stub with a file, maybe smeared a little grease on it, because I didn't even notice when I examined that gun. But I'm guessing that if Alvin pulls the trigger on that hog leg, even though it's loaded, the gun won't go off."

"Why would I do such a thing? Alvin is my friend."

"Yeah? I'll bet he's not your best friend. Maybe

Rita is."

We'd come to the end of the dirt road and were now on more civilized pavement. I had to slow down for the occasional motorist now that we were in a busier part of town. Milton made more than one hesitant move towards the passenger's door handle, but I didn't really think he'd jump.

"What do you mean by suggesting Rita is my best friend? Nothing improper, I hope."

"When I was checking the locks on the French doors in your bedroom tonight I caught a whiff of perfume in the general area of your bed."

"My personal life is none of your concern."

"Granted. But there was something familiar about the scent. It took me a while to remember where I'd sniffed it before. It's an unusual fragrance. I've only smelled it on one woman. Rita. Why would Rita be in your bedroom long enough, or often enough, to leave the smell of her perfume behind? I was wrong about your inclinations. I'm guessing you and Rita are lovers. I'm also guessing that you and Rita set up Alvin so you could blackmail him. Why? I'm guessing so he'd be willing to sign over some pretty valuable real estate to her. And I'm guessing his death will be the final seal to it."

"You're mad, do you know that? Demented. I insist you tell me where you're taking me."

"I don't have to. We're almost there."

No squad car had the decency to tail me, even though I ran three red lights. I was also pretty sure that Rita had never actually hired any security men to watch Alvin. I'd have to deal with things myself.

Only one light shone in Alvin's house as I pulled into his drive. A lamp in the living room. Like I'd figured, there was no sign of a security detail. As soon as I stepped out of the car a shot rang out from somewhere inside the house. I ran for the porch. I didn't bother with the front door, figuring it'd be locked. Instead, I kicked out most of the living room window, then took my hat and cleared out the shards of glass that still stuck out of the frame.

As I stepped over the sill I drew my thirty-eight from my waistband holster and headed for Alvin's den, thinking that's where he'd be, but when I came level with the doorway and looked in, the room was empty. That's when the second shot hit my ears.

I fired my thirty-eight at the ceiling, just to let folks know they had company, then I ran toward the back of the house where I thought the shot had come from. I made it through the kitchen and into a hallway where I saw someone wearing a slouch hat and a topcoat, and one of the ugliest faces I've ever seen. Roscoe. He pointed a big pistol at me and pulled the trigger.

Something smashed against my wrist, and then my left hand went numb. I aimed my thirty-eight at Roscoe's belly and squeezed off two shots. He went down. Something hit me in the back, just as I heard a lady-finger firecracker go off, then another. I turned around and there was that fool Milton pelting me with baby bullets from his purse gun. I sent a slug in his direction and he grabbed at his ribs and fell down. Things were pretty quiet after that. The show was over.

I began collecting stray guns and checking bullet holes. Milton had taken my bullet in his upper ribs, on the left side, a little below his armpit. He was hollering, but he wasn't bleeding much, and I thought he'd be OK.

As for Roscoe, well, of course it wasn't Roscoe. I pulled the mask off and there was Rita's lovely face, contorted with pain. One of my shots had missed her entirely, and the other one had broken her right arm, above the elbow. She was crying, and there was quite a bit of blood. I needed to get her to a hospital, but first I had to find out if Alvin was dead.

I found him on the floor beside his bed. One of Rita's shots must have missed him, but the other one had plugged him in the right side of his chest, probably puncturing a lung. He was passed out, but every breath he took made a sucking sound around the wound. Nobody was dead yet, but I wasn't sure how much longer that would be true.

As for me, I had a shattered wrist-watch, a swollen, possibly broken, wrist, and something that felt like a big mosquito bite a little to one side of my backbone. I found the phone in the living room, called the cops, and told them about the carnage. The dispatcher said it sounded kind of like something from Shakespeare and promised to send a squad car and call for an ambulance. I wanted another cigar.

The cops and the croaker's helpers showed up at exactly the same time. Lots of shiny lights and melodious sirens. The cops stayed behind in the house to try to figure out what had happened and whether or not any of us four gunshot victims were lying or hiding anything. There were a couple of ambulance attendants, plus the driver, and they all gave us a good looking over.

One guy, a young fellow, took a little more time fussing over Rita than I thought was justified, so I directed his attention to me. He pulled up my shirt in back, put a plaster on what was probably a gunshot wound from Milton's baby pistol, and then started fooling with my injured wrist. I would have had him check my broken watch, but that wasn't his specialty.

"Does it hurt when you do this?" He flopped his wrist up and down.

I flopped mine up and down. "Damn! It hurts like hell!"

"It hurts when you do this?" He flopped his hairy wrist again.

"Yeah, it hurts."

"Then don't do it."

Great, a comedian.

"What exactly happened here tonight?" he asked, wrapping my wrist in about a mile of bandage.

"Well, you know how it is. A few friends get together, drink a few Nesbitt's, play some Parcheesi, and the next thing you know all hell breaks loose."

"Parcheesi? Is that Russian?"

"I think it was invented in India."

"Sounds Russian. They have some dangerous games. Like Russian Roulette. You ever play that?"

"Sure, but I always wear a helmet. So how are my comrades? Doing OK?" I nodded my head in the direction on my wounded play fellows.

"Don't know yet. We got to get you all to the hospital. But there's no way the four of you will fit in the hearse — I mean, the ambulance."

This guy was a barrel of laughs. I volunteered to drive myself to Quartz Quarry General.

I walked out the door, resisting the urge to go back out through the broken window. By the time I reached my car I had counted five nosey neighbors, all stretching their necks to get peeks at the house. When I looked at them they all turned their eyes away in spite of my sweet smile. Standing right in front of my car was a dumpy couple dressed in bathrobes and pajamas. They had a dumpy little boy with them, also wearing night apparel.

"First gunfight, son?" I asked the kid, just to be amiable. He gave me a scared look and ducked behind his mom's broad rump.

"What exactly happened in there?" the man asked. He held an unlit briar pipe in one hand. It gave him a rather dashing appearance.

Before I could concoct an answer, a gravelly voice behind me growled, "OK folks, break it up. Show's over."

It was one of the cops. The stupid one. Or maybe it was the other stupid one. He waved his arms around like he was chasing chickens, then rested one hand on his holstered revolver, and the other one on the billy-club in his belt. The small crowd reluctantly backed out into the road.

"I got to go with you," the cop told me.

"What the hell for? I'm the good guy."

"Maybe you is and maybe you ain't. Don't matter. Orders. The chief is sending over another squad car and a couple more officers. Butch is staying here to hold down the fort. I got to escort the ambulance."

"Fine, escort them. I'll be right behind you."

"No you won't, you'll be right beside me. We're taking your car, and I'm driving. I got to leave the squad car for Butch in case he needs it."

"Listen, you can go with me, but you aren't driving my car. Nobody drives it but me."

"You're gunshot, in no shape to drive. Hand over the keys."

The keys were in the ignition where I'd left them during my hasty rescue mission, but I didn't tell the cop that. I just went around to the driver's side and got in. I'd barely started the buggy when the cop opened the passenger's door and lowered his bulk onto the seat. He slammed the door.

"Watch it!" I said. "This isn't your jalopy. You treat it with respect."

"Pardon me," he said, sarcasm dripping from his mouth like slaver from the jaws of a rabid mutt. "Go ahead, drive. Some folks are just too stubborn."

"Nobody ever called me that before."

I waited a minute until the ambulance was ready to haul its trophies to the hospital. When it finally got moving it put on quite a show. Blinking lights, blaring siren, and plenty of speed. The whole nine yards. I followed as best I could, but I have to admit my wrist was giving me trouble. I was leaning forward a little the whole way in case my bullet wound started leaking; I didn't want blood staining the upholstery.

The officer didn't like my driving.

"You shouldn't be going this fast, you're a civilian."

"So? Deputize me. If I slow down I'll lose that ambulance."

"Jeez, some guys you can't get along with no matter what. All right, you're deputized."

"Thanks, chief. I hope the power doesn't go to my head."

"Smart guy. Tell me something. What really went on back there at the OK Corral? Which one of them did you say you was working for?"

"I hate to admit it, but at the end of the farce I

was working for all of them."

"Yeah? Which one of them's going to pay you?"

"Don't make me think about it."

We hit a big dip in the road and the Hornet was airborne for a few exciting seconds.

"Watch it, will you?" the cop complained. "Damn, I wish this thing had a siren. Tell me something else. I'm confused. The dame with the mask, I know why she shot you, and I think I know why the fancy boy shot you. But, tell me, why did Copperhead plug the guy with the squeaky lung? What the hell did he do to any-body?"

"I believe that Copperhead, as you call her, thinks that Squeaky Lung may have been respon-sible for her mother-in-law's death."

"Come on, am I a chump? Why would anybody shoot someone for killing their mother-in-law?"

"Copperhead also fancies some swell property she got Squeaky Lung to sign over to her. She doesn't want him asking for it back after he di-vorces his wife"

By the time we pulled into the U-shaped drive behind the hospital my wrist was giving me fits. I found an out-of-the-way spot to park and escorted my escort into the emergency room. What I really wanted to do was go home. I'd even be willing to forgo the painkillers I needed to get home to my own bed.

But, as I've pointed out before, I'm awfully cu-rious by nature. I couldn't wait to find out how my fellow gunfighters were doing. Really, Alvin was the only one I thought might actually die. But you never know, Milton and Rita might be in danger too. Hospitals are no place to be if you're sick or hurt.

19

The late night emergency room was its usual bloody mess. Drunken car wreck victims, bar fight bleeders, nocturnal heart attack sufferers. And now, a gunshot gumshoe, a locksmith with a bullet in his lung, an artist with a broken rib or two, and a redheaded femme fatale with a shattered elbow.

That was the report I got when I finally captured a passing nurse while I waited for my own wounds to be tended. She was one of those cute little things that male patients love and female patients detest. Chestnut hair tucked under her cap, doe eyes, ruby lips, starched white curves. But her personality didn't live up to her looks. She didn't like my detaining her, even for a second. She had patients to torture.

"Your Chicago mob friends?" she said, with just a touch of acid. "Oh, they're fine. The one with the lead in his lung is almost perky. His lung's filling full of fluid, he has a broken rib, and he's lost a bathtub's worth of blood, but in a month or two he'll be up and at 'em. Trust me.

"As for the floozy, she'll never play the violin again, or even eat with a fork unless a couple of surgeries can fix things. And Little Lord Light-in-the-Loafer? Well — "

"Hey, don't call him that. What a guy does in the back seat of his car is his own damned business."

"Yeah? You like that type, do you?"

I leaned dangerously close to her. "I know of types I like a whole lot less, sister. How is he?"

"Fair to middling. They picked some rib-bone splinters out of his side, and there's some muscle damage. He'll live, and then some. Listen, I've got to go. They don't pay me to palaver with bums like you."

She swished her white skirts and showed me the backs of her white-stockinged legs as she walked away. And just when I was beginning to like her.

As for me, they gave me a couple of shots. One for tetanus and one for pain. They took a forceps and pried a pea-sized slug out of my back. They left the wound open to drain, and to stain my bed sheets later, though they did put a gauze patch on it. They spent more time on my wrist. They unwrapped it, exclaimed over the swelling and bruising, and insisted I have X-rays. I insisted they all go to hell. I rewrapped my wrist myself and walked out of the joint. Finally, I was going home.

I don't know what kind of pain killer they'd given me, but it had pretty well worn off by the time I finished the drive to my house. I knew I wasn't going to get any sleep for a while, so I made a pot of coffee and started pacing and thinking, in that order.

Why had Rita tried to kill Alvin? The idea that she was avenging Ethel still made sense to me, but only a little sense. There had to be something more. If Rita wanted to kill someone, she should have killed Roscoe.

I stopped pacing. That idea really got me to thinking. What if Rita had killed her husband? She had the means: Ethel's left-over pills. And she had the motives: fear and loathing. Rita could have slipped a little something special into Roscoe's breakfast pancakes the morning of the last day of his life, the morning he drove off to a golf tournament and ended up fishing instead. I liked the notion.

I went over each point carefully. First, Rita had concealed her knowledge of her husband's killings and she had failed to report his behavior to the authorities or to the medical community. Second, she went and poisoned the guy herself. Problem solved, right? But something else must have happened, something in just the last few months that made her want to kill Alvin. Maybe something that made him suspicious.

A little after dawn, the coffee, the pain, and the stimulating conversation I was having with myself, wore off. I fell asleep as soon as I'd crawled into bed. It was close to noon when I woke up. If anyone had called me, I'd slept through the ringing of the phone. I half expected to hear from the police, but the longer they left me alone the better. I made a new pot of coffee and contemplated a late breakfast. I was feeling kind of queasy, though, and decided I'd wait to eat until later. In the meantime, I could call Quartz Quarry General and see how the patients were faring. As for me, my wrist was no more swollen or bruised than it had been the night before. I considered that a good sign.

When I made my phone call to the hospital, I found out that my nasty little nurse of the night before had been correct in her assessments. Alvin would live, would likely recover entirely, but it would take time. Rita's broken arm was serious. Even though my bullet had struck her arm a little above the elbow, some splinters of bone, and maybe bullet fragments, had penetrated her elbow joint. Surgery was definitely in her future. She might not ever recover the full use of her arm.

I tried not to feel sorry, rotten, guilty, but it was no use. I felt all those things. I couldn't help it. Milton would likely be the first to be released. His broken ribs and torn muscles were painful, but not serious. I bet he wished he'd taken the rest of his brandy to the hospital with him.

By two o'clock I was getting hungry enough to ignore my belly queasy. I considered fixing something myself, but I don't like my cooking even when I'm feeling well. I needed to find a nice quiet restaurant and order something soothing, like a bowl of cream soup with those tiny oyster crackers they always give you. I got into the Hudson and headed for town.

On the way I did some more thinking about Rita and her crimes, and her motives. A further piece of knowledge that Alvin didn't have yet was who was behind the blackmail scheme that Milton had confessed to. Once Alvin heard that Rita had been in on it, and that she was also Milton's lover, things could get pretty dicey for Rita. It was all beginning to add up, at least I thought so. But if Rita was ever going to get nailed for her crimes, a whole lot would have to be revealed that was largely in darkness now. And I was the right guy to make that happen.

There was no one parked directly in front of Rocko's, so I took the spot. I was about to get out of the car when a thought froze me and kept me behind the wheel for a moment. Tracy had told me she never had a day off, but I knew it couldn't be true: what if this was her day off? If I went inside and some attractive, polite, competent waitress greeted me, I wouldn't know how to act. I'd have to go someplace else.

When I finally walked in the door, the smell of stale grease and week-old pastry hit me in the nose like a boxing glove. I looked toward the counter and there she was, sour-faced as ever, in a wrinkled smock and a silly hat that was supposed to make her look professional.

"Sinbad the Sailor!" she greeted me. "Where you been all this time?"

"It's only been a day or two," I said, taking my usual stool. "How you been?"

"Swell. What happened to you? You're hurt."

How could she know? I'd thrown a sports coat on before leaving home so that my bandaged wrist wouldn't show, and she certainly couldn't see the bullet hole in my back. "I'm fine. A little under the weather is all."

"Don't try to lie to Aunty Tracy. You're hurt. Here, I'll make fresh coffee for you. Tell me all about it."

"I don't know why I'm even telling you this. I got in a gunfight last night."

"Naw! Now you're lying."

I took off my jacket and laid it across the counter. That was a mistake, but it was too late. By now my jacket likely had enough grease on it to let me use it as a raincoat. Tracy saw the wrapped bandage on my wrist.

"Who did that, an ape?"

"You can't even see it yet. Let me take off the bandage."

"That's what I meant. Who wrapped you up, an ape?"

"Hey," I growled, "I did that myself."

"So, I was right. Let me see what's under it. Your coffee's almost done."

I carefully unwound the bandage, which was already getting dirty, and revealed my multi-colored, twice-its-regular-size, wrist. It looked hairier than usual, too. Tracy turned as white as an angel's baby teeth.

"That's broken. You should have a cast. Didn't you go to a doctor, tough guy?"

"I went to the hospital last night. You satisfied? I'll be fine."

She poured me a cup of coffee, but her hand was shaking, and she didn't spill a drop. This was a first.

"You telling me a bullet did that?"

"Kind of. It hit my watch."

"Boy, I'll bet that watch is going to be in the shop for a while."

"I've got a bullet hole in my back, too."

"You don't say? Let me see it."

"No. What do you think this is, a locker room? What if somebody walks in?"

Tracy snorted. "Nobody comes in here. That's why we always have leftovers to sell the next day. Let me see it. Come on."

I swiveled on my stool until my back was to her. She untucked my shirt in back, pulled it up, and carefully peeled the gauze away from my wound. She gasped. "Land o' Goshen!" she said. "Sorry. Pardon my French. That looks like an hon-est-to-God bullet hole."

"Tuck my shirt back in," I grumbled. She did so, and I turned back around and got an eyeful of the menu. That reminded me I was hungry. "You got any soup? Something gentle and creamy?"

"Gentle and creamy? Do you know where you are? This is Rocko's. We've got chili. You got a gimpy tummy? From all those bullets?"

"Sort of. Give me a bowl of chili, with some of those little oyster crackers."

"Oysters we've got, canned, but no oyster crackers. We've got saltines, or graham crackers."

"Saltines, and another cup of coffee."

"Coming right up, but you've got to tell me all about what happened last night. How many bad guys did you kill?"

The chili made me sick as a dog, which is probably the kind of meat it was made from. Tracy kept me talking for half an hour about my late-night escapades. But I had nothing else to do; I no longer had a client. I'd be lucky if I even got paid.

I drove over to my office to see what was going on. The place smelled even mustier than usual, and there was a big fan-shaped heap of mail on the floor. The correspondence was as dismal as usual: bills, flyers, more bills. I needed another case, and soon. I sat at my desk and briskly opened and filed my mail. Advertisements in the trash, duns in my biggest desk drawer. When I was through, I smoked a cigar.

For the three hours I made myself stay in my office, the phone rang once. Somebody wanting Sylvia. I told him I wasn't named Sylvia and I didn't know any Sylvias. He called me a liar and hung up. A little later I gave up, grabbed my hat, and headed for the old homestead. My wrist was stiff and sore, but I thought I could detect a slight diminishment in the swelling. I certainly had an easier time manipulating the steering wheel.

The whole time I was driving, and even after I'd reached home, I kept thinking about the Ravencamp case. I didn't want to let it go, and it wasn't just because of the money I was owed. Actually, I was pretty sure Alvin would cover the tab, if he lived. I had questions I wanted answered, and the person I wanted to talk to first was Alvin. I needed to know what he knew. Then maybe I'd talk to Rita. Possibly even Milton. But first, I needed to sleep.

Instead of speaking to Alvin, I spent the next couple of days getting grilled by the cops. I gave them everything I had. What the hell? But the whole experience made me long for my office. I could be clearing away cobwebs or doing my filing.

When I was finally told I could visit Alvin, I hustled the Hornet over to Quartz Quarry General. I was told at the nurses' station that Milton had already been released and taken directly to jail.

Rita, on the other hand, was still in the hospital, but could not receive visitors. When I passed her room on my way down the hall to Alvin's room, a burly police woman was seated on a folding chair in front of Rita's closed door. She gave me a move-along-buster look, so I moved along.

Alvin's door was open. The room had two beds, but the other bed was unoccupied. Alvin was propped up on pillows. He had a pile of padlocks on the bed sheet and was working on one of them with a couple of lock picks. He looked up when I came in, smiled with apparent pleasure, and said, "Hey, it's my favorite detective. The best investigator in the whole wide world." There was no sarcasm in his voice. "You caught me killing time picking locks. You can never have too much practice."

"How's it going, Alvin? You going to live?"

"You bet. I'm feeling great, really. One of these days they'll let me out of this pen. Everybody's been nice, though. The doctors, the nurses. Say, before I get sidetracked, let me take care of something. I had one of my employees stop by my house to pick up some personal stuff for me and to bring these locks for me to practice on. You know, my own toothbrush, my razor, my wallet and checkbook." He looked at me expectantly.

"Yeah?"

"I want to pay you. I don't know if Rita's ever going to come up with her half of the payment. I kind of doubt it. That's OK, I'll be happy to pay the whole tab myself. Delighted, and I ain't kidding. Have you got the final bill ready?"

"Yeah. We can go over the expenses any time you feel up to it."

He waved my words away. "I trust you." He

pointed to a white metal cabinet near one side of his bed. "Look in the second drawer down. My checkbook's there, and a pen. Get them for me, will you?"

"We don't have to do this right now. I didn't come up here to badger you about paying me."

"No time like the present. Hell, I'm sure you can use the money."

Boy, was that the truth. I fetched the checkbook and pen and handed them to the patient. "You sure you're up to writing? How's the lung?"

"They drained it, and patched it, and it's OK. I don't have all my breath back, and my chest still hurts, but I'm doing pretty good." He started writing on a check blank. "Give me the bad news. How much?"

I gave him the bad news. He didn't even blink. He finished filling out the check, tore it from the book, and handed it to me. He'd made a mistake. It was fifty dollars too much. I looked at him and opened my mouth. He started laughing, but the laugh turned into a cough.

"Hell, I got to get used to laughing again. That extra fifty's my gift to you, and it ain't enough. You saved my bacon. You saved my life, pal."

I snorted. "Saved your bacon? I almost cooked your goose. If it'd taken me five minutes longer to figure things out you'd be in the boneyard right now."

"That don't matter. You did figure things out. I didn't have a clue what was going on. And to think that Rita and Milton — " He didn't finish his sentence, just shook his head.

"Let me ask you something, if you don't mind."

"Shoot. I got all the time in the world."

"Do you know why Rita and Milton wanted you dead?"

20

He picked up one of his padlocks and started playing with it. "Not for sure. I don't know for sure."

"But you've got ideas. You have to."

"I can't talk to you about it. There's secrets involved. Family secrets. I'm sorry, Axe, but that's the way it is."

I was sitting in a small, uncomfortable chair near his bedside. I leaned forward. "I know some of those secrets already. Maybe all of them. Do you want me to tell you what I know, and what I've guessed?"

He was all ears. I told him about Roscoe's taste for hunting human prey, Ethel's possible suicide, Rita and Milton's affair. I even threw in my idea about Rita murdering Roscoe. By the time I was finished talking, Alvin was looking a lot more like a hospital patient than when I'd first walked into his room. What seemed to bother him most was Rita's having slept with Milton, and having been part of the blackmail scheme.

"You sure aren't making me feel any better, Axe. Jeez, it's even worse than I thought. You know, when I woke up in the emergency room, I didn't exactly know what had happened. I knew somebody who looked like my brother had shot me. But I also knew it wasn't really Roscoe. Too small, and I had an idea his face was a mask. But Rita? And I thought, why? Sure, I knew she blamed me a little for my mom's death, but I didn't seriously believe she thought Mom had killed herself on purpose.

"As for the rest, the blackmail partnership with Milton, and her sleeping with him, I didn't know any of that. Not until you told me just now. You sure about it?" He wrinkled his brow. "Of course you're sure. You're the best investigator in the world." This time there was a trace of sarcasm in his voice. "As for her poisoning Roscoe, don't be silly. And my knowing about it?" He shook his head and gave me a sad look of pity.

That made me mad. "Look, Alvin, I want Rita and Milton to pay for what they've done. If I can't get your help, then I'll do it on my own. But if that's the case, I'll run rough-shod over you to put those two in jail where they belong. You understand? You've already got yourself in trouble protecting family secrets. Come clean. You'll feel better.

"The two of us haven't always gotten along, but I still consider you a basically decent guy. Stop lying. Admit to Della you've had an affair. Your marriage is already over and you know it. Stop lying about Roscoe, about the way he lived, and the way he died. You're not going to get in much trouble, if any. But if Rita and Milton walk away from all this without serving jail time, there won't be any second chance to make them pay for their sins."

"Now you sound like a priest."

"Sure, call me Father Axe. What do you say? Are you going to spill what you know?"

He thought about it. He fussed with his locks some more, and gave me a couple of hard looks. "All right, I'll tell you. But if none of this stuff has to be brought up in court, then I don't want you telling anybody about it. Deal?"

"Sure. Deal."

"You're right about the way Roscoe died. It might not have been an ordinary car accident. I was over at Roscoe and Rita's house the morning of the golf tournament. Milton was there too, damn him. It wasn't unusual for the four of us to get together on weekends for meals after Della left me and took the kids. On this occasion, Rita and Milton put together a great breakfast."

"I knew it — I knew the guy could cook."

"Yeah. Rita too. Anyway, there were pancakes, and eggs, and toast, and bacon, and a special kind of sausage that Rita always bought for Roscoe. The rest of us didn't care that much for it — it was too spicy. Roscoe loved it. Now, you know, he was getting ready for a golf tournament. He usually ate like a pig at times like that. He said he needed extra food to keep his strength up. But on this particular day he only ate two sausage patties, instead of his usual three or four, though he ate everything else in sight.

"I asked him if there was something wrong with it and he said it tasted kind of stale. That didn't make any sense. So, anyway, I ate part of a patty myself just to see what he was talking about. It didn't taste stale to me, but there was definitely something wrong with it. And I couldn't help but feel that both Rita and Milton were acting kind of nervous somehow. I felt tired after the meal, but I thought it was because I ate too much, so I didn't think anything more about it until Roscoe drove his car into the river. Then I got to wondering.

"I knew Rita was scared of Roscoe because of what he'd done to those hunters, and because he knew she knew about it. I couldn't imagine she'd kill him though. Rita? I tried not to think about it. But it kept bothering me.

"Finally, I guess it was a couple of months ago, I brought the subject up to her. I told her I'd been having some really bad headaches lately but I didn't want to bother going to a doctor. I asked her if she knew what had happened to Mom's pills, the one's she'd had in her house when she died. Rita told me she'd thrown them all out. OK. But later, when I happened to go to the can, I snooped around in the medicine cabinet in Roscoe and Rita's bathroom.

"There were two bottles of Mom's pills, both almost empty. I didn't know what to think. If she'd drugged Roscoe with Mom's pills, wouldn't she get rid of the rest of them just in case somebody got suspicious? But then, why did she lie to me about having thrown them out? Didn't that mean she was trying to hide something?

"I asked her about it, and she told me she forgot she had them. Then a month later, I saw Roscoe, or thought I did." Alvin shrugged. "I'm some kind of idiot. I should have figured it out.

"Anyhow, that's all I know. I swear. And now you're telling me she cheated on me while I was cheating on Della. What a world. Poor Della. When I told her about my brother's killing hunters, she ran to her sister's with the kids and stayed for months. When I told her, about six weeks ago, that Rita may have killed Roscoe, well, she took it hard. I don't think she's coming back, ever."

"Thanks for coughing up the truth. I'll keep my promise to you. I won't spill the beans unless I have to."

"Thanks."

"I guess I ought to be going. Anything I can bring you the next time I visit?"

"Some magazines maybe. These padlocks are starting to bore me."

When I left Alvin, I walked back the way I'd come in hopes of catching at least a glimpse of a tousled Rita on her bed of pain. I don't know why

I wanted to see her, I just did. But when I drew close to her room I saw that the police woman was still guarding her prisoner, and this time she had re-enforcements. The cop I'd driven to the hospital was standing next to the lady cop's chair, with a goofy grin on his face. When he saw me he stepped into my path to block my way.

"Well, if it ain't the gumshoe with the lead foot." He was a big guy, and he had struck his favorite pose, one hand on the butt of his revolver and the other on the knob of his billy club. But at least he was smiling, two gold teeth showing. He motioned with his thick-fingered hand to stop me. "Say, Marge," he addressed his compatriot, "me and the shamus here are going to the automat for a bite. Want anything?"

"Bring me back a couple of sandwiches, tuna salad if they got."

We started down the hall together and had gotten no more than thirty feet when Officer Marge called out to us.

"Oh, Cream Puff? Bring me back something to drink, too, will you?"

"Cream Puff?" I whispered to my cop.

"Shut up," he said. "That's just her name for me."

"What do you call her?"

"None of your damned business."

We took an elevator down two floors and walked a short distance to a good-sized room featuring plain tables, without cloths, and a bunch of folding chairs. One wall was pretty much taken up by the automat, rows of little glass doors winking in the light from the ceiling fixtures.

"So, what'd you bring me down here for, officer?"

"Biff. The name's Biff Munson" We shook hands. "I brought you down here to buy you lunch, you sap. I owe you."

"How do you figure?"

"Marge. Officer Ringo. Used to be she wouldn't give me the time of day. Treated me like I was the invisible man. Then you had that little shootout at your pal's place, and I was in on the investigation. All of a sudden Marge is treating me like I'm the best thing since sliced pumpernickel. She's got all these questions for me. And now we're, you know, sweeties."

"Congratulations."

"Hey, thanks. It couldn't have happened without you, so I figure I at least owe you lunch."

"That's not necessary, but I guess I could use a bite."

He pulled a handful of change out of his pocket and dumped about half of it into my palm.

"Get whatever you want."

While Biff went around slipping quarters into slots like he was in a casino, I took my time perusing the cornucopia of foodstuffs. They didn't have any egg sandwiches, but they did have one made with egg salad. I bought it. Then I picked out some cold baked beans, a container of pineapple juice, and a slice of Boston cream pie for dessert.

I joined Biff at a table where he had amassed a stack of five or six sandwiches, some potato salad, some macaroni salad, some triple layer chocolate cake, and a slice of lemon meringue pie. He was already busy wolfing down a sandwich, lubricating it with gulps of tomato juice, when I sat down. I pushed the leftover change to his side of the table.

"Don't forget to save some for Marge," I said.

His mouth full, he answered me by patting a couple of tuna salad sandwiches he'd set aside next to a container of lemonade. While he attacked his food like he belonged to the locust family, I ate my lunch more daintily.

Everything went down swell except the egg salad sandwich. I don't know what kind of bird laid those eggs, but I hope I never meet one in a dark alley. By the time I'd finished my meal Biff was through eating and ready to talk.

"What brought you to the hospital today?" I asked. "Just visiting Marge?"

He shook his head. "No. The Chief Detective's here. I'm his driver for today. Can you believe it? Some guys are so uppity and important they can't do their own driving. Oh, well, I ain't complaining."

"What's he here for?"

"Talking to Copperhead again. He's been here twice before."

"Rita giving him problems?"

Biff laughed. "Naw, she ain't giving no problems. She's been singing like a parakeet. Both her and Rembrandt have been squawking like crows."

"Rembrandt?"

"You know, the artist guy that potted you in the back."

"I can't see either Rita or Milton singing to the police. What gives?"

"After we hit them both with the information you gave us, they went for each other's throats like — what's the saying? — like a couple of constipated badgers. They been giving up all their secrets, hoping to hurt each other."

"You think they're hanging themselves? I don't mean that literally. You think they're providing evidence that could put them both in jail?"

Biff nodded, wiped some meringue from his fat lips. "They're making it easy for us. All we're going to have to do is unlock the cell doors and shoo them in. Trust me, Copperhead and Rembrandt are headed to the big house."

I stood up and shook hands with Biff. "Officer Munson, you've made my day, and I thank you for lunch."

"You're welcome. Thanks for playing Cupid."

I let that remark slide and headed for the hospital exit.

21

Thanks to Alvin I had a nice fat check in my billfold. I stopped by my bank, deposited the check, and took out some cash. Then I drove to a nearby men's clothing store and parked in their lot. A bright young fellow met me at the front door with a big smile on his face.

"I see you're here for a complete new outfit, sir. Come this way, we have everything."

"I just want a tie, the rest will have to wait. Do you have neckties?"

His smile almost disappeared. "Of course. Right this way."

I followed him over to a couple of circular racks of all kinds and colors of ties. This was going to be a hard decision. I went through about fifty of them and finally found the one I wanted. It was a wide lemon yellow silk affair, with a pattern of tiny orange giraffes. I loved it, but I wasn't certain it was tasteful. I turned to the clerk, who was still hovering in the area. "Is this tie tasteful?"

He looked up, blinked. "All our ties are tasteful, sir. It's part of our guarantee. That tie goes extremely well with your eyes."

"OK, I was just checking. I guess I'll take it."

"Splendid. Anything else today? We have a lovely sports coat that would go perfectly with that tie. And if we don't have your exact size, we offer free alterations."

"Just the tie today, thanks."

I followed the guy to the cash register and he rang me up. God, the thing was expensive! I should have looked at the price before I decided to buy it. But it was for a good cause. I returned to the Hornet and laid the tie down on the passenger's seat.

On the way to my destination I thought of something else. Flowers. Where could I find a flower shop? There must be one around here somewhere. I was driving through a residential area and passed an old clapboard house with a nice garden out front.

There were some rows of yellow tulips right near the curb. And further back in the yard grew some kind of orange-colored flowers. I stopped the car and then backed up a ways. A woman pushing sixty or thereabouts, and wearing a baggy green housedress, was out in the garden watering stuff with a long garden hose. She jumped when I honked the horn.

"Excuse me," I bellowed. "I don't suppose you know where there's a flower shop in these parts?"

She turned down the nozzle of her hose and slowly approached my car. "I don't believe there are any flower shops in this part of town. Why do you ask?"

I thought about lying to her, making up a dying-grandma-who-loved-tulips story, or something. But then I just went with the truth. "Here's the problem. I'm going to be asking out this swell girl, and I'm on my way to see her, but I'm running late. Like a sap, I forgot to get flowers to take her. I don't suppose you'd consider selling me three or four of yours? I like the yellow tulips, and those orange things back there. Yellow and orange are her favorite colors."

She smiled. "Those are poppies. I won't sell you any, but I'll give you a few for such a worthy cause."

"I can't tell you how swell that'd be. Thanks."

"Let me run get my clippers."

"I've got my jackknife."

"Jackknives aren't for cutting delicate flowers. I'll only be a moment."

She went to the front porch and returned with a small pair of gardening shears. With them she harvested two tulips and two poppies and brought them out to me.

"Are you sure I can't pay you something for these? You got me out of a jam."

She smiled again. "No charge. Tell your sweetheart hello, and treat her decently."

Sweetheart, I thought, as I drove away. I bet she

wouldn't call Tracy that if she met her. In no time I was back at Rocko's. The space out front was vacant, just like yesterday. That was good, it meant there likely weren't any diners inside. I didn't want eavesdroppers when I asked Tracy out to dinner. I put on my new tie, giving it my best Windsor knot, though it hurt my sore wrist to do it. I felt pretty spiffy.

Tracy was standing behind the counter, chewing gum, and assaulting the countertop with her beloved mildewed rag when I walked in.

"Two days in a row?" she asked. "That's like having two Christmases."

"OK. Merry Christmas."

"And a Happy New Year to you. More chili? There's some in the pot."

"Keep it, I'm not here to eat. But I wouldn't mind a cup of Joe. Fresh, if possible."

"Come on, I just made a fresh pot early this morning. It's not even three. You'll put us out of business."

"What a tragedy."

She set about making fresh coffee. "Who're the flowers for, your parole officer?"

"Kind of. They're for you."

She turned and gave me a hard stare. "What's the gimmick, sport?"

"No gimmick. I thought you might be more likely to agree to go out to dinner with me if I gave you flowers first."

"I've got a shotgun behind this counter, you

know."

"Yeah, I've seen it. Not much of a piece. Put these in some water why don't you?" I stuck the flowers in her face.

She grabbed them and dunked them down in a half-finished glass of iced tea that some customer had left on the counter.

"You'll kill them," I complained.

"Tea's got caffeine. It'll keep them awake."

She didn't say another word until the coffee was cooked and she'd slopped some in a cup for me.

"Thanks," I said.

"Surely."

"So is it a yes, or a no? I'll take you some place swell, I swear. The Blue Ox if you want."

"Why me? Just tell me that."

"Don't make me think about it. Yes or no?"

"The food at the Blue Ox would kill me. I'm used to eating here."

"You told me you never ate the food here."

"I only told you that so you wouldn't lose respect for me. In school we read a story called 'Rappaccini's Daughter.' Ever hear of it?"

"I read it when I was in jail."

"You were in jail? Say, you'll have to play the harmonica for me sometime. Anyway, I'm like the girl in that story. I'm so used to eating bad food that if I ever went out and ate good food I'd die."

"Don't worry, you can order the worst thing on the menu. If it's too edible when they bring it out we'll send it back and have them ruin it."

"You're a sap."

"I'll say. When can I pick you up? When do you get off work?"

"Nine."

"Why so late? I can't take you out to dinner after nine."

"We get some of our best business around seven or eight. It's when other restaurants are already closed and hungry folks don't have any choice but to come to Rocko's."

"OK, then when's your next day off? Don't lie to me again and try to claim you don't get days off."

"Tomorrow. I get one day off a week, and it's tomorrow."

"Then count on me picking you up at six. Got that? By the way, where do you live?"

Tracy made a hitchhiking gesture at the ceiling.

"You really live above this dump?"

"It makes the drive to work nice and short. What should I wear for this silly date?"

"Your best fairy princess outfit."

"Oh, come on, I don't want to wear my work clothes."

"Wear something nice, whatever you've got."

"Are you going to wear that tie?" She pointed a stubby digit at my spanking new necktie.

"I like this tie. I bought it special. What's wrong with it?"

"Nothing. It's divine. I just don't want you

spilling anything on it. Maybe you could wear something more practical, like a rubber bib."

"Sure, that'll go nice with your high chair."

I didn't want to eat at Rocko's; I'd already had lunch, so I told Tracy goodbye.

"Don't forget I'm picking you up at six tomorrow. Wear your frilliest dress."

"Don't worry. I'll look like Cinderella, only before her fairy godmother showed up."

The Hornet was looking pretty dirty. I hadn't been treating it right lately. I stopped at Pop's Pro Pump, a gas station that offered car washes. I watched out the window of the waiting room while a couple of guys in blue coveralls soaped and rinsed my ride. They also swept out the interior. One of the guys came into the station and walked over to me.

"Your misses must have dropped this," he told me. He had a voice like transmission gears stripping.

"What is it?" He dropped something into my palm, and I looked at it. It was a gold earring with an emerald stone the color of Rita's eyes. I remembered she'd worn these earrings when we'd gone to the Italian restaurant.

"Found it on the floorboards in front. Bet your old lady will be happy to get it back." The guy winked.

"Thanks," I said.

I turned it over in my palm. I figured I'd hang on to it, and if Rita ever got out of prison I'd give it back to her. In the meantime, it'd make a nice memento. I like having souvenirs of all my cases. The earring would look good with the stuffed armadillo, the blood-stained flat iron, the sequined slipper, and the Captain Hook hand puppet.

END

If you have enjoyed this book, please go to its Amazon book page and leave a short review. It will be most appreciated!

OTHER BOOKS BY THIS AUTHOR:

GLIMMER IN A GLASS EYE
[ISBN: 978-1-940469-02-7]

After 1950s gumshoe Axel Hatchett is hired to protect a used car dealer from a threat of murder, Hatchett finds himself in a nest of rattlesnakes — literally! When the car dealer is bumped off, and Hatchett's prime suspect is murdered, the sleuth is forced to sift through a deck of also-ran suspects to solve the two killings before another corpse is added. And to make matters worse, he's falling for a mouthy waitress who works in a sleazy diner....

SLAYER IN A GRAY TOUPEE
[ISBN: 978-1-940469-01-0]

Rumpled 1950s sleuth, Axel Hatchett, is summoned to the Flinders Mansion to prevent a millionaire's threatened murder. After a fierce blizzard knocks out the power and closes the roads, Hatchett is trapped in the candle-lit mansion with an eccentric array of terrified guests and servants. The detective is determined to solve the case, but his only clue is a sinister gray toupee.

THREE CURSING BIRDS
[ISBN: 978-1-940469-03-4]

When thieves snatch a statue of the bird-headed Egyptian god, Thoth, and drop its owner from a third-story window, 1950s private detective Axel Hatchett is set on their trail. But wait! – there are actually three statues, and one of them may contain a treasure map! Hatchett enlists the aid of his hash-slinging fiancée and a snake-handling English professor to help solve the case of the three cursed birds.

KILLER BEAR FOR HIRE
[ISBN: 978-1-940469-04-1]

In all his years of sleuthing, snarky 1950s private eye Axel Hatchett has never faced a case like this: a bear trained to kill. Hatchett finds himself hunted by a deadly two-legged predator whose bullet comes unnervingly close to Hatchett's new wife, and that has Hatchett seeing red! Armed with a revolver and his caustic wits, Hatchett is out to solve a grizzly killing, or die trying.

BOOK CLUB DISCUSSION QUESTIONS
(For People Who Didn't Skip Over the Dull Parts)

1. How did you experience this book? Were you engaged immediately or did you fall asleep immediately?

2. Describe the main characters — their personality traits, motivations, inner qualities. Did any of the characters remind you of your irritating next-door neighbor?

3. Was the plot engaging — did the story interest you? Did you decide to watch T.V. instead of finishing the book?

4. What main ideas — themes — does the author explore? Any? I sure didn't see any.

5. What passages struck you as insightful, even profound? Well, never mind that. Did you find the book funny? Yes? Do you also find the average phone directory funny?

6. Was the ending satisfying? If so, why? If not, why not? Were you hoping that all the characters would die in a horrible natural disaster?

7. Did this novel change you? Are you easily changed? Do you change as often as you change your socks?

8. What was the author trying to accomplish (provide entertainment for the reader, deliver a message, or earn enough money to make a down payment on a British-racing-green Bentley?)

9. Would you buy another novel by this author? Why?

10. Did this book remind you of Gone With The Wind? It did? Explain.

ABOUT THE AUTHOR

Steven LeRoy Nelson is an award-winning humorist whose short fiction has appeared in *Alfred Hitchcock Mystery Magazine, Ellery Queen Mystery Magazine, The Leviathan,* and numerous other publications.

Visit him at his website at:

www.stevenleroynelson.com

www.ingramcontent.com/pod-product-compliance
Lightning Source LLC
Chambersburg PA
CBHW030129180626
46812CB00002B/622